Hawaika was a paradise planet, where soft warm winds breathed across the dreaming seas of the evening of a world. But Terran Time Agents Ross Murdock and Gordon Ashe knew that Hawaika's past held the key to a power riddle which reached across hundreds of galaxies—and eons of time.

When they set up their time probe, they got much more than they'd bargained for—for they were catapulted back in time into the middle of a fantastic battle that raged in the seas and on the shores of Hawaika, a combat of alien forces which not even the ancient peoples of Hawaika understood.

Marooned in the planet's past, they found themselves drawn into the climactic struggle whose disastrous outcome they knew to be inevitable.

# KEY OUT OF TIME

ANDRE NORTON

A Division of Charter Communications Inc.
A GROSSET & DUNLAP COMPANY
51 Madison Avenue
New York, New York 10010

KEY OUT OF TIME



An Ace Book, by arrangement with
The World Publishing Co.



This Printing: February 1981
Printed in U.S.A.
Published Simultaneously in
Canada

# I

# LOTUS WORLD

THERE WAS a shading of rose in the pearl arch of sky, deepening at the horizon meeting of sea and air in a rainbow tint of cloud. The lazy swells of the ocean held the same soft color, darkened with crimson veins where spirals of weed drifted. A rose world bathed in soft sunlight, knowing only gentle winds, peace, and—sloth.

Ross Murdock leaned forward over the edge of the rock ledge to peer down at a beach of fine sand, pale pink sand with here and there a glitter of crystalline "shell"—or were those delicate, fluted ovals shells? Even the waves came in languidly. And the breeze which ruffled his hair, smoothed about his sun-browned, half-bare body, caressed it, did not buffet on its way inland to stir the growths which the Terran settlers called "trees" but which possessed long lacy fronds instead of true branches.

Hawaika—named for the old Polynesian paradise—a world seemingly without flaw except the subtle one of being too perfect, too welcoming, too wooing. Its long, uneventful, unchanging days enticed forgetfulness, offered a life without effort. Except for the mystery . . .

Because this world was not the one pictured on the tape which had brought the Terran settlement team here. A map, a directing guide, a description all in one, that was the ancient voyage tape. Ross himself had helped to loot a storehouse on an unknown planet for a cargo of such tapes. Once they had been the space-navigation guides for a race or races who had ruled the star lanes ten thousand years in his own world's past, a civilization which had long since sunk again into the dust of its beginning.

Those tapes, returned to Terra after their chance discovery, were studied, probed, deciphered by the best brains of his time, shared out by lot between already suspicious Terran powers, bringing into the exploration of space bitter rivalries and old hatreds.

Such a tape had landed their ship on Hawaika, a world of shallow seas and archipelagoes instead of true continents. The settlement team had had all the knowledge contained on that tape crowded into them, only to discover that much they had learned from it was false!

Of course, none of them had expected to discover here still the cities, the civilization the tape had projected as existing in that long-ago period. But no present island string they had visited approximated those on the maps they had seen, and so far they had not found any trace that any intelligent beings had walked, built, lived, on these beautiful, slumberous atolls. So, what had happened to the Hawaika of the tape?

Ross's right hand rubbed across the ridged scars which disfigured his left one, to be carried for the rest of his life as a mark of his meeting with the star voyagers in the past of his own world. He had deliberately seared his own flesh to break the mental control they had asserted. Then the battle had gone to him. But from it he had brought another scar—the unease of that old terror when Ross Murdock, fighter, rebel, outlaw by the conventions of his own era, Ross Murdock, who considered himself an exceedingly tough individual, that toughness steeled by the training for Time Agent sorties, had come up against a power he did not understand, instinctively hated and feared.

Now he breathed deeply of the wind—the smell of the sea, the scents of the land growths, strange but pleasant. So easy to relax, to drop into the soft, lulling swing of this world in which they had found no fault, no danger, no irritant. Yet, once those others had been here—the blue-suited, hairless ones he called "Baldies." And what had happened then . . . or afterward?

A black head, brown shoulders, slender body, broke the sleepy slip of the waves. A shimmering mask covered the face, catching glitter-fire in the sun. Two hands freed a chin curved yet firmly set, a mouth made more for laughter than sternness, wide dark eyes. Karara Trehern of the Alii, the one-time Hawaikan god-chieftain line, was an exceedingly pretty girl.

But Ross regarded her aloofly, with a coldness which bordered on hostility, as she flipped her mask into its pocket on top of the gill-pack. Below his rocky perch she came to a halt, her feet slightly apart in the sand, an impish twist to her lips as she called mockingly:

"Why not come in? The water's fine."

"Perfect, like all the rest of this." Some of his impatience came out in the sour tone. "No luck, as usual?"

"As usual," Karara conceded. "If there ever was a civilization here, it's been gone so long we'll probably never find any traces. Why don't you just pick out a good place to set up that time-probe and try it blind?"

Ross scowled. "Because"—his patience was exaggerated to the point of insult—"we have only one peep-probe. Once it's set we can't tear it down easily for transport somewhere else, so we want to be sure there's something to look at beyond."

She began to wring the water out of her long hair. "Well, as far as we've explored . . . nothing. Come yourself next time. Tino-rau and Taua aren't particular; they like company."

Putting two fingers to her mouth, Karara whistled. Twin heads popped out of the water, facing the shore and her. Projecting noses, mouths with upturned corners so they curved in a lasting pleasant grin at the mammals on the shore—the dolphin pair, mammals whose ancestors had chosen the sea, whistled back in such close counterfeit of the girl's signal that they could be an echo of her call. Years earlier their species' intelligence had surprised, almost shocked men. Experiments, training, co-operation, had developed a tie which gave the water-limited race of mankind new eyes, ears, minds, to see, evaluate, and report concerning an element in which the bipeds were not free.

Hand in hand with that co-operation had gone other experiments. Just as the clumsy armored diving suits of the early twentieth century had allowed man to begin penetration into a weird new world, so had the frog-man equipment made him still freer in the sea. And now the gill-pack which separated the needed oxygen from the water made even that lighter burden of tanks obsolete. But there remained depths into which man could not descend, whose secrets were closed to him. There the dolphins operated, in a partnership of minds, equal minds—though that last fact had been difficult for man to accept.

Ross's irritation, unjustified as he knew it to be, did not rest on Tino-rau or Taua. He enjoyed the hours when he buckled on gill-pack and took to the sea with those two ten-foot, black-and-silver escorts sharing the action. But Karara . . . Karara's presence was a different matter altogether.

The Agents' teams had always been strictly masculine. Two men partnered for an interlocking of abilities and temperaments, going through training together, becoming two halves of a strong and efficient whole. Before being summarily recruited into the Project, Ross had been a loner—living on the ragged edges of the law, an indigestible bit for the civilization which had become too ordered and "adjusted" to absorb his kind. But in the Project he had discovered others like himself—men born out of time, too ruthless, too individualistic for their own age, but able to operate with ease in the dangerous paths of the Time Agents.

And when the time search for the wrecked alien ships had succeeded and the first intact ship found, used, duplicated, the Agents had come from forays into the past to be trained anew for travel to the stars. First there had been Ross Murdock, criminal. Then there had been Ross Murdock and Gordon Ashe, Time Agents. Now there was still Ross and Gordon and a quest as perilous as any they had known. Yet this time they had to depend upon Karara and the dolphins.

"Tomorrow"—Ross was still not sorting out his thoughts, truly aware of the feeling which worked upon him as a thorn in the finger—"I will come."

"Good!" If she recognized his hostility for what it was, that did not bother her. Once more she whistled to the dolphins, waved a casual farewell with one hand, and headed up the beach toward the base camp. Ross chose a more rugged path over the cliff.

Suppose they did not find what they sought near here? Yet the old taped map suggested that this was approximately the site starred upon it. Marking a city? A star port?

Ashe had volunteered for Hawaika, demanded this job after the disastrous Topaz affair when the team of Apache volunteers had been sent out too soon to counter what might have been a Red sneak settlement. Ross was still unhappy over the ensuing months when only Major Kelgarries and maybe, in a lesser part, Ross had kept Gordon Ashe in the Project at all. That Topaz had been a failure was accepted when the settlement ship did not return. And that had added to Ashe's sense of guilt for having recruited and partially trained the lost team.

Among those dispatched over Ashe's vehement protests had been Travis Fox who had shared with Ashe and Ross the first galactic flight in an age-old derelict space-ship. Travis Fox—the Apache archaeologist—had he ever reached Topaz? Or would he and his team wander forever between worlds? Did they set down on a planet where some inimical form of native life or a Red settlement had awaited them? The very uncertainty of their fate continued to ride Ashe.

So he insisted on coming out with the second settlement team, the volunteers of Samoan and Hawaiian descent, to carry on a yet more exciting and hazardous exploration. Just as the Project had probed into the past of Terra, so would Ashe and Ross now attempt to discover what lay in the past of Hawaika, to see this world as it had been at the height of the galactic civilization, and so to learn what they could about their fore-runners into space. And the mystery they had dropped into upon landing added to the necessity for that discovery or discoveries.

Their probe, if fortune favored them, might become a gate through time. The installation was a vast improvement over these passage points they had first devised. Technical information had taken a vast leap forward after Terran engineers and scientists had had access to the tapes of the stellar empire. Adaptations and short-cuts developed, so that a new hybrid technology came into use, woven from the knowledge and experimentation of two civilizations thousands of years apart in time.

If and when he or Ashe—or Karara and her dolphins—discovered the proper site, the two Agents could set up their own equipment. Both Ross and Ashe had had enough drill in the process. All they needed was the brick of discovery; then they could build their wall. But they must find some remainder of the past, the smallest trace of ancient ruin upon which to center their peep-probe. And since landing here the long days had flowed into weeks with no such discovery made.

Ross crossed the ridge of rock which formed a cocks-comb rise on the island's spine and descended to the village. As they had been trained, the Polynesian settlers adapted native products to their own heritage of building and tools. It was necessary that they live off the land, for their transport ship had had storage space only for a limited number of supplies and tools. After it took off to return home they would be wholly on their own for several years. Their ship, a silvery ball, rested on a rock ledge, its pilot and crew having lingered to learn the results of Ashe's search. Four days more and they would have to lift for home even if the Agents still had only negative results to report.

That disappointment was driving Ashe, the way that six months earlier his outrage and guilt feelings over the Topaz affair had driven him. Karara's suggestion carried weight the longer Ross thought about it. With more swimmers hunting, there was just that much increased chance of turning up some clue. So far the dolphins had not reported any dangerous native sea life or any perils except the natural ones any diver always had at his shoulder under the waves.

There were extra gill-packs, and all of the settlers were good swimmers. An organized hunt ought to shake the Polynesians out of their present do-it-tomorrow attitude. As long as they had had definite work before them—the unloading of the ship, the building of the village, all the labors incidental to the establishing of this base—they had shown energy and enthusiasm. It was only during the last couple of weeks that the languor which appeared part of the atmosphere here had crept up on them, so that now they were content to live at a slower and lazier pace. Ross remembered Ashe's comparison made the evening before, likening Hawaika to a legendary Terran island where the inhabitants lived a drugged existence, feeding upon the seeds of a native plant. Hawaika was fast becoming a lotus land for Terrans.

"Through here, then westward . . ." Ashe hunched over the crate table in the mat-walled house. He did not look up as Ross entered. Karara's still damp head was bowed until those black locks, now sleeked to her round skull, almost touched the man's close-cropped brown hair. They were both studying a map as if they saw not lines on paper but the actual inlets and lagoons which that drawing represented.

"You are sure, Gordon, that this *is* the modern point to match the site on the tape?" The girl brushed back straying hair.

Ashe shrugged. There were tight brackets about his mouth which had not been there six months ago. He moved jerkily, not with the fluid grace of those old days when he had faced the vast distance of time travel with unruffled calm and a self-confidence to steady and support the novice Ross.

"The general outline of these two islands could stand for the capes on this—" He pulled a second map, this on transparent plastic, to fit over the first. The capes marked on the much larger body of land did slip over the modern islands with a surprising fit. The once large island, shattered and broken, could have produced the groups of atolls and islets they now prospected.

"How long—" Karara mused aloud, "and why?"

Ashe shrugged. "Ten thousand years, five, two." He shook his head. "We have no idea. It's apparent that there must have been some world-wide cataclysm here to change the contours of the land masses so much. We may have to wait on a return space flight to bring a 'copter or a hydroplane to explore farther." His hand swept beyond the boundaries of the map to indicate the whole of Hawaika.

"A year, maybe two, before we could hope for that," Ross cut in. "Then we'll have to depend on whether the Council believes this important enough." The contrariness which spiked his tongue whenever Karara was present made him say that without thinking. Then the twitch of Ashe's lip brought home Ross's error. Gordon needed reassurance now, not a recitation of the various ways their mission could be doomed.

"Look here!" Ross came to the table, his hand sweeping past Karara, as he used his forefinger for a pointer. "We know that what we want could be easily overlooked, even with the dolphins helping us to check. This whole area's too big. And you know that it is certain that whatever might be down there would be hidden with sea growths. Suppose ten of us start out in a semi-circle from about here and go as far as this point, heading inland. Video-cameras here and here . . . comb the whole sector inch by inch if we have to. After all, we have plenty of time and manpower."

Karara laughed softly. "Manpower—always manpower, Ross? But there is woman-power, too. And we have perhaps even sharper sight. But this is a good idea, Gordon. Let me see—" she began to tell off names on her fingers, "PaKeeKee, Vaeoha, Hori, Liliha, Taema, Ui, Hono'ura—they are the best in the water. Me . . . you, Gordon, Ross. That makes ten with keen eyes to look, and always there are Tino-rau and Taua. We will take supplies and camp here on this island which looks so much like a finger crooked to beckon. Yes, somehow that beckoning finger seems to me to promise better fortune. Shall we plan it so?"

Some of the tight look was gone from Ashe's face, and Ross relaxed. This was what Gordon needed—not to be sitting in here going over maps, reports, reworking over and over their scant leads. Ashe had always been a field man; and the settlement work had been stultifying, a laborious chore for him.

When Karara had gone Ross dropped down on the bunk against the side wall.

"What *did* happen here, do you think?" Half was real interest in the mystery they had mulled over and over since they had landed on a Hawaika which diverged so greatly from the maps; the other half, a desire to keep Ashe thinking on a subject removed from immediate worries. "An atomic war?"

"Could be. There are old radiation traces. But these aliens had, I'm sure, progressed beyond atomics. Suppose, just suppose, they could tamper with the weather, with the balance of the planet's crust? We don't know the extent of their powers, how they would use them. They had a colony here once, or there would have been no guide tape. And that is all we are sure of."

"Suppose"—Ross rolled over on his stomach, pillowed

his head on his arms—"we could uncover some of that knowledge—"

The twitch was back at Ashe's lips. "That's the risk we have to run now."

"Risk?"

"Would you give a child one of those hand weapons we found in the derelict?"

"Naturally not!" Ross snapped and then saw the point. "You mean—*we* aren't to be trusted?"

The answer was plain to read in Ashe's expression.

"Then why this whole setup, this hunt for what might mean trouble?"

"The old pinch, the bad one. What if the Reds discover something first? They drew some planets in the tape lottery, remember. It's a seesaw between us—we advance here, they there. We have to keep up the race or lose it. They must be combing their stellar colonies for a few answers just as furiously as we are."

"So, we go into the past to hunt if we have to. Well, I think I could do without answers such as the Baldies would know. But I will admit that I would like to know what did happen here—two, five, ten thousand years ago."

Ashe stood up and stretched. For the first time he smiled. "Do you know, I rather like the idea of fishing off Karara's beckoning finger. Maybe she's right about that changing our luck."

Ross kept his face carefully expressionless as he got up to prepare their evening meal.

## II

## LAIR OF MANO NUI

JUST UNDER the surface of the water the sea was warm, weird life showed colors Ross could name, shades he could not. The corals, the animals masquerading as plants, the plants disguised as animals which inhabited the oceans of Terra, had their counterparts here. And the settlers had given them the familiar names, though the crabs, the fish, the anemones, and weeds of the shallow lagoons and reefs were not identical with Terran creatures. The trouble was that there was too much, such a wealth of life to attract the eyes, hold attention, that it was difficult to keep to the job at hand—the search for what was not natural, for what had no normal place here.

As the land seduced the senses and bewitched the off-worlder, so did the sea have its enchantment to pull one from duty. Ross resolutely skimmed by a forest of weaving, waving lace which varied from a green which was almost black to a pale tint he could not truly identify. Among those waving fans lurked ghost-fish, finned swimmers transparent enough so that one could sight, through their pallid sides, the evidences of recently ingested meals.

The Terrans had begun their sweep-search a half hour ago, slipping overboard from a ferry canoe, heading in toward the checkpoint of the finger isle, forming an arc of expert divers, men and girls so at home in the ocean that they should be able to make the discovery Ashe needed—if such did exist.

Mystery built upon mystery on Hawaika, Ross thought

as he used his spear-gun to push aside a floating banner of weed in order to peer below its curtain. The native life of this world must always have been largely aquatic. The settlers had discovered only a few small animals on the islands. The largest of which was the burrower, a creature not unlike a miniature monkey in that it had hind legs on which it walked and forepaws, well clawed for digging purposes, which it used with as much skill and dexterity as a man used hands. Its body was hairless and it was able to assume, chameleonlike, the color of the soil and rocks where it denned. The head was set directly on its bowed shoulders without vestige of neck; and it had round bubbles of eyes near the top of its skull, a nose which was a single vertical slit, and a wide mouth fanged for crushing the shelled creatures on which it fed. All in all, to Terran eyes, it was a vaguely repulsive creature, but as far as the settlers had been able to discover it was the highest form of land life. The smaller rodentlike things, the two species of wingless diving birds, and an odd assortment of reptiles and amphibians sharing the island were all the burrowers' prey.

A world of sea and islands, what type of native intelligent life had it once supported? Or had this been only a galactic colony, with no native population before the coming of the stellar explorers? Ross hovered above a dark pocket where the bottom had suddenly dipped into a saucer-shaped depression. The sea growth about the rim rippled in the water raggedly, but there was something about its general outline. . . .

Ross began a circumference of that hollow. Allowing for the distortion of the growths which had formed lumpy excrescences or reached turrets toward the surface —yes, allowing for those—this was decidedly something out of the ordinary! The depression was too regular, too even. Ross was certain of that. With a thrill of excitement he began a descent into the cup, striving to trace signs which would prove his suspicion correct.

How many years, centuries, had the slow coverage of the sea life gathered there, flourished, died, with other creatures to build anew on the remains? Now there was only a hint that the depression had other than a natural beginning.

Anchoring with a one-handed grip on a spike of Hawaikan coral—smoother than the Terran species—Ross aimed the butt of his spear-gun at the nearest wall of the saucer, striving to reach into a crevice between two lumps of growth and so probe into what might lie behind. The spear rebounded; there was no breaking that crust with such a fragile tool. But perhaps he would have better luck lower down.

The depression was deeper than he had first judged. Now the light which existed in the shallows vanished. Red and yellow as colors went, but Ross was aware of blues and greens in shades and tints which were not visible above. He switched on his diving torch, and color returned within its beam. A swirl of weed, pink in the light, became darkly emerald beyond as if it possessed the chameleon ability of the burrowers.

He was distracted by that phenomenon, and so he transgressed the diver's rule of never becoming so absorbed in surroundings as to forget caution. Just when did Ross become aware of that shadow below? Was it when a school of ghost-fish burst unexpectedly between weed growths, and he turned to follow them with the torch? Then the outer edge of his beam caught the movement of a shape, a flutter in the water of the gloomy depths.

Ross swung around, his back to the wall of the saucer, as he aimed the torch down at what was arising there. The light caught and held for a long moment of horror something which might have come out of the nightmares of his own world. Afterward Ross knew that the monster was not as large as it seemed in that endless minute of fear, perhaps no bigger than the dolphins.

He had had training in shark-infested seas on Terra,

been carefully briefed against the danger from such hunters of the deep and ocean jungles. But this kind of thing had only existed before in the fairy tales of his race as the dragon of old lore. A scaled head with wide eyes gleaming in the light beam with cold and sullen hate, a gaping mouth fang-filled, a horn-set muzzle, that long, undulating neck and, below it, the half-seen bulk of monstrous body.

His spear-gun, the knife at his waist belt, neither were protection against this! Yet to turn his back on that rising head was more than Ross could do. He pulled himself back against the wall of the saucer. The thing before him did not rush to attack. Plainly it had seen him and now it moved with the leisure of a hunter having no fears concerning the eventual outcome of the hunt. But the light appeared to puzzle it and Ross kept the beam shining straight into those evil eyes.

The shock of the encounter was wearing off; now Ross edged his flipper into a crevice to hold him steady while his hand went to the sonic-com at his waist. He tapped out a distress call which the dolphins could relay to the swimmers. The swaying dragon head paused, held rigid on a stiff, scaled column in the center of the saucer. That sonic vibration either surprised or bothered the hunter, made it wary.

Ross tapped again. The belief that if he tried to escape, he was lost, that only while he faced it so had he any chance, grew stronger. The head was only inches below the level of his flippered feet as he held to the weeds.

Again that weaving movement, the rise of head, a tremor along the serpent neck, an agitation in the depths. The dragon was on the move again. Ross aimed the light directly at the head. The scales, as far as he could determine, were not horny plates but lapped, silvery ovals such as a fish possessed. And the underparts of the monster might even be vulnerable to his spear. But knowing the way a Terran shark could absorb the darts of that weapon and survive, Ross feared to attack except as a last resort.

Above and to his left there was a small hollow where in the past some portion of the growths had been ripped away. If he could fit himself into that crevice, perhaps he could keep the dragon at bay until help arrived. Ross moved with all the skill he had. His hand closed upon the edge of the niche and he whirled himself up, just making it into that refuge as the head lashed at him wickedly. His suspicion that the dragon would attack anything on the run was well founded, and he knew he had no hope of winning to the surface above.

Now he stood in the crevice, facing outward, watching the head darting in the water. He had switched off the torch, and the loss of light appeared to bewilder the reptile for some precious seconds. Ross pulled as far back into the niche as he could, until the point of one shoulder touched a surface which was sleek, smooth, and cold. The shock of that contact almost sent him hurtling out again.

Gripping the spear before him in his right hand, Ross cautiously felt behind him with the left. His fingertips glided over a seamless surface where the growths had been torn or peeled away. Though he could not, or dared not, turn his head to see, he was certain that this was his proof that the walls of the saucer had been fashioned and placed there by some intelligent creature.

The dragon had risen, hovering now in the water directly before the entrance to Ross's hole, its neck curled back against its bulk. The body, sloping from a massive round of shoulders to a tapering rear, was vaguely familiar. If one provided a Terran seal with a gorgon head and scales in place of fur, the effect would be similar. But Ross was assuredly not facing a seal at this moment.

Slight movement of the flippers kept it as stabilized as if it sprawled on a supporting surface. With the neck flattened against the body, the head curved downward until the horn on its snout pointed the tip straight at Ross's middle. The Terran steadied his spear-gun. The dragon's eyes were its most vulnerable targets; if the creature launched the attack, Ross would aim for them.

Both man and dragon were so intent upon their duel that neither was conscious of the sudden swirl overhead. A sleek dark shape struck down, skimming across the humped-back ridge of the dragon. Some of the settlers had empathy with the dolphins to a high degree, but Ross's own powers of contact were relatively feeble.

Only now he was given an assurance of aid, and a suggestion to attack. The dragon head writhed, twisted as the reptile attempted to see above and behind its own length. But the dolphin was only a streak fast disappearing. And that writhing changed the balance the monster had maintained, pushing it toward Ross.

The Terran fired too soon and without proper aim, so the dart snaked past the head. But the harpoon line half-hooked about the neck and seemed to confuse the creature. Ross squirmed as far back as he could into his refuge and drew his knife. Against those fangs the weapon was an almost useless toy, but it was all he had.

Again the dolphin dived in attack on the reptile, this time seizing in its mouth the floating cord of the harpoon and giving it a jerk which jolted the dragon even more off balance, pulling it away from Ross's niche and out into the center of the saucer.

There were two dolphins in action now, Ross saw, playing the dragon as matadors might play a bull, keeping the creature disturbed by their agile maneuvers. Whatever prey came naturally to the Hawaikan monster was not of this type, and the creature was not prepared to deal effectively with their teasing, dodging tactics. Neither had touched the beast, but they kept it constantly striving to get at them.

Though it swam in circles attempting to face its teasers, the dragon did not abandon the level before Ross's refuge, and now and then it darted its head at him, unwilling to give up its prey. Only one of the dolphins frisked and dodged above now as the sonic on Ross's belt vibrated against his lower ribs with its message warning to be prepared for further action. Somewhere above, his own kind gathered. Hurriedly he tapped out in code his warning in return.

Two dolphins busy again, their last dive over the dragon pushing the monster down past Ross's niche toward the saucer's depths. Then they flashed up and away. The dragon was rising in turn, but coming to meet the Hawaikan creature was a ball giving off light, bringing sharp vision and color with it.

Ross's arm swung up to shield his eyes. There was a flash; such answering vibration carried through the waves that even his nerves, far less sensitive than those of the life about him, reacted. He blinked behind his mask. A fish floated by, spiraling up, its belly exposed. And about him growths drooped, trailed lifelessly through the water; while there was now a motionless bulk sinking to the obscurity of the depression floor. A weapon perfected on Terra to use against sharks and barracuda had worked here to kill what could have been more formidable prey.

The Terran wiggled out of the niche, rose to meet another swimmer. As Ashe descended, Ross relayed his news via the sonic. The dolphins were already nosing into the depths in pursuit of their late enemy.

"Look here—" Ross guided Ashe to the crevice which had saved him, aimed the torch beam into it. He had been right! There was a long groove in the covering built up by the growths; a vertical strip some six feet long, of a uniform gray, showed. Ashe touched the find and then gave the alert via the sonic code.

"Metal or an alloy, we've found it!"

But what did they have? Even after an hour's exploration by the full company, Ashe's expert search with his knowledge of artifacts and ancient remains, they were still baffled. It would require labor and tools they did not have, to clear the whole of the saucer. They could be sure only of its size and shape, and the fact that its walls were of an unknown substance which the sea could cloak but not erode. For the length of gray surface showed not the slightest pitting or time wear.

Down at its centermost point they found the dragon's den, an arch coated with growth, before which sprawled the body of the creature. That was dragged aloft with the dolphins' aid, to be taken ashore for study. But the arch itself . . . was that part of some old installation?

Torches to the fore, they entered its shadow, only to remain baffled. Here and there were patches of the same gray showing in its interior. Ashe dug the butt of his spear-gun into the sand on the flooring to uncover another oval depression. But what it all signified or what had been its purpose, they could not guess.

"Set up the peep-probe here?" Ross asked.

Ashe's head moved in a slow negative. "Look farther . . . spread out," the sonic clicked.

Within a matter of minutes the dolphins reported new remains—two more saucers, each larger than the first, set in a line on the ocean floor, pointing directly to Karara's Finger Island. Cautiously explored, these were discovered to be free of any but harmless life; they stirred up no more dragons.

When the Terrans came ashore on Finger Island to rest and eat their midday meal one of the men paced along the beached dragon. Ashore it lost none of its frightening aspect. And seeing it, even beached and dead, Ross wondered at his luck in surviving the encounter without a scratch.

"I think that this one would be alone," PaKeeKee commented. "Where there is an eater of this size, there is usually only one."

"Mano-Uui!" The girl Taema shivered as she gave to this monster the name of the shark demon of her people. "Such a one is truly king shark in these waters! But why have we not sighted its like before? Tino-rau, Taua . . . they have not reported such—"

"Probably because, as PaKeeKee says, these things are rare," Ashe returned. "A carnivore of its size would have to have a fairly wide hunting range, yet there's evidence that this thing has laired in that den for some time. Which means that it must have a defined hunting territory allowing no trespassing from others of its species."

Karara nodded. "Also it may hunt only at intervals, eat heavily, and lie quiet until that meal is digested. There are large snakes on Terra that follow that pattern. Ross was in its front yard when it came after him—"

"From now on"—Ashe swallowed a quarter of fruit—"we know what to watch for, and the weapon which will finish it off. Don't forget that!"

The delicate mechanisms of their sonics had already registered the vibrations which would warn of a dragon's presence, and the depth globes would then do the rest.

"Big skull, oversize for the body." PaKeeKee squatted on his heels by the head lying on the sand at the end of the now fully extended neck.

Ross had heretofore been more aware of the armament of that head, the fangs set in the powerful jaws, the horn on the snout. But PaKeeKee's comment drew his attention to the fact that the scale-covered skull did dome up above the eye pits in a way to suggest ample brain room. Had the thing been intelligent? Karara put that into words:

"Rule One?" She went over to survey the carcass.

Ross resented her half question, whether it was addressed to him or mere thinking aloud on her part.

Rule One: Conserve native life to the fullest extent. Humanoid form may not be the only evidence of intelligence.

There were the dolphins to prove that point right on Terra. But did Rule One mean that you had to let a monster nibble at you because it might just be a high type of alien intelligence? Let Karara spout Rule One while backed into a crevice under water with that horn stabbing at her mid-section!

"Rule One does not mean to forego self-defense," Ashe commented mildly. "This thing is a hunter, and you can't stop to apply recognition techniques when you are being regarded as legitimate prey. If you are the stronger, or an equal, yes—stop and think before becoming aggressive. But in a situation like this—take no chances."

"Anyway, from now on," Karara pointed out, "it could be possible to shock instead of kill."

"Gordon"—PaKeeKee swung around—"what have we found here—besides this thing?"

"I can't even guess. Except that those depressions were made for a purpose and have been there for a long time. Whether they were originally in the water, or the land sank, that we don't know either. But now we have a site to set up the peep-probe."

"We do that right away?" Ross wanted to know. Impatience bit at him. But Ashe still had a trace of frown. He shook his head.

"Have to make sure of our site, very sure. I don't want to start any chain reaction on the other side of the time wall."

And he was right, Ross was forced to admit, remembering what had happened when the galactics had discovered the Red time gates and traced them forward to their twentieth-century source, ruthlessly destroying each station. The original colonists of Hawaika had been as giants to Terran pygmies when it came to technical knowledge. To use even a peep-probe indiscreetly near one of their outposts might bring swift and terrible retribution.

## III

## THE ANCIENT MARINERS

ANOTHER MAP spread out and this time pinned down with small stones on beach gravel.

"Here, here, and here—" Ashe's finger indicated the points marked in a pattern which flared out from three sides of Finger Island. Each marked a set of three undersea depressions in perfect alliance with the land which, according to the galactic map, had once been a cape on a much larger land mass. Though the Terrans had found the ruins, if those saucers in the sea could be so termed, the remains had no meaning for the explorers.

"De we set up here?" Ross asked. "If we could just get a report to send back . . ." That might mean the difference between awakening the co-operation of the Project policy makers so that a flood of supplies and personnel would begin to head their way.

"We set up here," Ashe decided.

He had selected a point between two of the lines where a reef would provide them with a secure base. And once that decision was made, the Terrans went into action.

Two days to go, to install the peep-probe and take some shots before the ship had to clear with or without their evidence. Together Ross and Ashe floated the installation out to the reef, Ui and Karara helping to tow the equipment and parts, the dolphins lending pushing noses on occasion. The aquatic mammals were as interested as the human beings they aided. And in water their help was invaluable. Had dolphins developed hands, Ross wondered fleetingly, would they have long ago wrested control of their native world—or at least of its seas—from the human kind?

All the human beings worked with practiced ease, even while masked and submerged, to set the probe in place, aiming it landward at the check point of the Finger's protruding nail of rock. After Ashe made the final adjustments, tested each and every part of the assembly, he gestured them in.

Karara's swift hand movement asked a question, and Ashe's sonic code-clicked in reply: "At twilight."

Yes, dusk was the proper time for using a peep-probe. To see without risk of being sighted in return was their safeguard. Here Ashe had no historical data to guide him. Their search for the former inhabitants might be a long drawn-out process skipping across centuries as the machine was adjusted to Terran time eras.

"When were they here?" Back on shore Karara shook out her hair, spread it over her shoulders to dry. "How many hundred years back will the probe return?"

"More likely thousands," Ross commented. "Where will you start, Gordon?"

Ashe brushed sand from the page of the notebook he had steadied against one bent knee and gazed out at the reef where they had set the probe.

"Ten thousand years—"

"We know that galactic ships crashed on Terra then. So their commerce and empire—if it was an empire—was far-flung at that time. Perhaps they were at the zenith of their civilization; perhaps they were already on the down slope. I do not think they were near the beginning. So that date is as good a starting place as any. If we don't hit what we're after, then we can move forward until we do."

"Do you think that there ever was a native population here?"

"Might have been."

"But without any large animals, no modern traces of any," she protested.

"Of people?" Ashe shrugged. "Good answers for both. Suppose there was a world-wide epidemic of proportions to wipe out a species. Or a war in which they used forces beyond our comprehension to alter the whole face of this planet, which did happen—the alteration, I mean. Several things could have removed intelligent life. Then such species as the burrowers could have developed or evolved from smaller, more primitive types."

"Those ape-things we found on the desert planet." Ross thought back to their first voyage on the homing derelict. "Maybe they had once been men and were degenerating. And the winged people, they could have been less than men on their way up—"

"Ape-things . . . winged people?" Karara interrupted. "Tell me!"

There was something imperious in her demand, but Ross found himself describing in detail their past adventures, first on the world of sand and sealed structures where the derelict had rested for a purpose its involuntary passengers had never understood, and then of the Terrans' limited exploration of that other planet which might have been the capital world of a far-flung stellar empire. There they had made a pact with a winged people living in the huge buildings of a jungle-choked city.

"But you see"—the Polynesian girl turned to Ashe when Ross had finished—"you did find them—these ape-things and the winged people. But here there are only the dragons and the burrowers. Are they the start or the finish? I want to know—"

"Why?" Ashe asked.

"Not just because I am curious, though I am that also, but because we, too, must have a beginning and an end. Did we come up from the seas, rise to know and feel and think, just to return to such a beginning at our end? If your winged people were climbing and your ape-things descending"—she shook her head—"it would be frightening to hold a cord of life, both ends in your hands. Is it good for us to see such things, Gordon?"

"Men have asked that question all their thinking lives, Karara. There have been those who have said no, who have turned aside and tried to halt the growth of knowledge here or there, attempted to make men stand still on one tread of a stairway. Only there is that in us which will not stop, ill-fitted as we may be for the climbing. Perhaps we shall be safe and untroubled here on Hawaika if I do not go out to that reef tonight. By that action I may bring real danger down on all of us. Yet I can not hold back for that. Could you?"

"No, I do not believe that I could," she agreed.

"We are here because we are of those who must know—volunteers. And being of that temperament, it is in us always to take the next step."

"Even if it leads to a fall," she added in a low tone.

Ashe gazed at her, though her own eyes were on the sea where a lace of waves marked the reef. Her words were ordinary enough, but Ross straightened to match Ashe's stare. Why had he felt that odd instant of uneasiness as if his heart had fluttered instead of beating true?

"I know of you Time Agents," Karara continued. "There were plenty of stories about you told while we were in training."

"Tall tales, I can imagine, most of them." Ashe laughed, but his amusement sounded forced to Ross.

"Perhaps. Though I do not believe that many could be any taller than the truth. And so also I have heard of that strict rule you follow, that you must do nothing which might alter the course of history. But suppose, suppose here that the course of history could be altered, that whatever catastrophe occurred might be averted? If that was done, what would happen to our settlement in the here and now?"

"I don't know. That is an experiment which we have never dared to try, which we won't try—"

"Not even if it would mean a chance of life for a whole native race?" she persisted.

"Alternate worlds then, maybe." Ross's imagination caught up that idea. "Two worlds from a change point in history," he elaborated, noting her look of puzzlement. "One stemming from one decision, another from the alternate."

"I've heard of that! But, Gordon, if you could return to the time of decision here and you had it in your power to say, 'Yes—live!' or 'No—die!' to the alien natives, what would you do?"

"I don't know. But neither do I think I shall ever be placed in that position. Why do you ask?"

She was twisting her still damp hair into a pony tail and tying it so with a cord. "Because . . . because I feel . . . No, I can not really put it into words, Gordon. It is that feeling one has on the eve of some important event—anticipation, fear, excitement. You'll let me go with you tonight, please! I want to see it—not the Hawaika that is, but that other world with another name, the one they saw and knew!"

An instant protest was hot in Ross's throat, but he had no time to voice it. For Ashe was already nodding.

"All right. But we may have no luck at all. Fishing in time is a chancy thing, so don't be disappointed if we don't turn up that other world. Now, I'm going to pamper these old bones for an hour or two. Amuse yourselves, children." He lay back and closed his eyes.

The past two days had wiped half the shadows from his lean, tanned face. He had dropped two years, three, Ross thought thankfully. Let them be lucky tonight, and Ashe's cure could be nearly complete.

"What do you think happened here?" Karara had moved so that her back was now to the wash of waves, her face more in the shadow.

"How do I know? Could be any of ten different things."

"And will I please shut up and leave you alone?" she countered swiftly. "Do you wish to savor the excitement then, explore a world upon world, or am I saying it right? We have Hawaika One which is a new world for us; now there is Hawaika Two which is removed in time, not distance. And to explore that—"

"We won't be exploring it really," Ross protested.

"Why? Did your agents not spend days, weeks, even months of time in the past on Terra? What is to prevent your doing the same here?"

"Training. We have no way of learning the drill."

"What do you mean?"

"Well, it wasn't as easy as you seem to think it was back on Terra," he began scornfully. "We didn't just stroll through one of those gates and set up business, say, in Nero's Rome or Montezuma's Mexico. An Agent was physically and psychologically fitted to the era he was to explore. Then he trained, and how he trained!" Ross remembered the weary hours spent learning how to use a bronze sword, the technique of Beaker trading, the hypnotic instruction in a language which was already dead centuries before his own country existed. "You learned the language, the customs, everything you could about your time and your cover. You were letter perfect before you took even a trial run!"

"And here you would have no guides," Karara said, nodding. "Yes, I can see the difficulty. Then you will just use the peep-probe?"

"Probably. Oh, maybe later on we can scout through a gate. We have the material to set one up. But it would be a strictly limited project, allowing no chance of being caught. Maybe the big brains back home can take peep-data and work out some basis of infiltration for us from it."

"But that would take years!"

"I suppose so. Only you begin to swim in the shallows, don't you—not by jumping off a cliff!"

She laughed. "True enough! However, even a look into the past might solve part of the big mystery."

Ross grunted and stretched out to follow Ashe's example. But behind his closed eyes his brain was busy, and he did not cultivate the patience he needed. Peep-probes were all right, but Karara had a point. You wanted more than a small window into a mystery, you wanted a part in solving it.

The setting of the sun deepened rose to red, made a dripping wine-hued banner of most of the sky, so that under it they moved in a crimson sea, looked back at an island where shadows were embers instead of ashes. Three humans, two dolphins, and a machine mounted on a reef which might not even have existed in the time they sought. Ashe made his final adjustments, and then his finger pressed a button and they watched the vista-plate no larger than the palms of two hands.

Nothing, a dull gray nothing! Something must have gone wrong with their assembly work. Ross touched Ashe's shoulder. But now there were shadows gathering on the plate, thickening, to sharpen into a distinct picture.

It was still the sunset hour they watched. But somehow the colors were paler, less red and sullen than the ones about them in the here and now. And they were not seeing the isle toward which the probe had been aimed; they were looking at a rugged coastline where cliffs lifted well above the beach-strand. While on those cliffs—! Ross had not realized Karara had reached out to grasp his arm until her nails bit into his flesh. And even then he was hardly aware of the pain. Because there was a building on the cliff!

Massive walls of native rock reared in outward defenses, culminating in towers. And from the high point of one tower the pointed tail of a banner cracked in the wind. There was a headland of rock reaching out, not toward them but to the north, and rounding that . . .

"War canoe!" Karara exclaimed, but Ross had another identification:

"Longboat!"

In reality, the vessel was neither one nor the other, not the double canoe of the Pacific which had transported warriors on raid from one island to another, or the shield-hung warship of the Vikings. But the Terrans were right in its purpose: That rakish, sharp-prowed ship had been fashioned for swift passage of the seas, for maneuverability as a weapon.

Behind the first nosed another and a third. Their sails were dyed by the sun, but there were devices painted on them, and the lines of those designs glittered as if they had been drawn with a metallic fluid.

"The castle!" Ashe's cry pulled their attention back to land.

There was movement along those walls. Then came a flash, a splash in the water close enough to the lead ship to wet her deck with spray.

"They're fighting!" Karara shouldered against Ross for a better look.

The ships were altering course, swinging away from land, out to sea.

"Moving too fast for sails alone, and I don't see any oars." Ross was puzzled. "How do you suppose . . ."

The bombardment from the castle continued but did not score any hits. Already the ships were out of range, the lead vessel off the screen of the peep as well. Then there was just the castle in the sunset. Ashe straightened up.

"Rocks!" he repeated wonderingly. "They were throwing rocks!"

"But those ships, they must have had engines. They weren't just depending on sails when they retreated." Ross added his own cause for bewilderment.

Karara looked from one to the other. "There is something here you do not understand. What is wrong?"

"Catapults, yes," Ashe said with a nod. "Those would fit periods corresponding from the Roman Empire into the Middle Ages. But you're right, Ross, those ships had power of some kind to take them offshore that quickly."

"A technically advanced race coming up against a more backward one?" hazarded the younger man.

"Could be. Let's go forward some." The incoming tide was washing well up on the reef. Ashe had to don his mask as he plunged head and shoulders under water to make the necessary adjustment.

Once more he pressed the button. And Ross's gasp was echoed by one from the girl. The cliffs again, but there was no castle dominating it, only a ruin, hardly more than rubble. Now, above the sites of the saucer depressions great pylons of silvery metal, warmed into fire brilliance by the sunset, raked into the sky like gaunt, skeleton fingers. There were no ships, no signs of any life. Even the vegetation which had showed on shore had vanished. There was an atmosphere of stark abandonment and death which struck the Terrans forcibly.

Those pylons, Ross studied them. Something familiar in their construction teased his memory. That refuel planet where the derelict ship had set down twice, on the voyage out and on their return. That had been a world of metal structures, and he believed he could trace a kinship between his memory of those and these pylons. Surely they had no connection with the earlier castle on the cliff.

Once more Ashe ducked to reset the probe. And in the fast-fading light they watched a third and last picture. But now they might have been looking at the island of the present, save that it bore no vegetation and there was a rawness about it, a sharpness of rock outline now vanished.

Those pylons, were they the key to the change which had come upon this world? What were they? Who had set them here? For the last Ross thought he had an answer. They were certainly the product of the galactic empire. And the castle . . . the ships . . . natives . . . settlers? Two widely different eras, and the mystery still lay between them. Would they ever be able to bring the key to it out of time?

They swam for the shore where Ui had a fire blazing and their supper prepared.

"How many years lying between those probes?" Ross pulled broiled fish apart with his fingers.

"That first was ten thousand years ago, the second," Ashe paused, "only two hundred years later."

"But"—Ross stared at his superior—"that means—"

"That there was a war or some drastic form of invasion, yes."

"You mean that the star people arrived and just took over this whole planet?" Karara asked. "But why? And those pylons, what were they for? How much later was that last picture?"

"Five hundred years."

"The pylons were gone, too, then," Ross commented. "But why—?" he echoed Karara's question.

Ashe had taken up his notebook, but he did not open it. "I think"—there was a sharp, grim note in his voice—"we had better find out."

"Put up a gate?"

Ashe broke all the previous rules of their service with his answer:

"Yes, a gate."

## IV

## STORM MENACE

"WE HAVE to know," Ashe leaned back against the crate they had just emptied. "Something was done here—in two hundred years—and then, an empty world."

"Pandora's box." Ross drew a hand across his forehead, smearing sweat and fine sand into a brand.

Ashe nodded. "Maybe we run that risk, loosing all the devils of the aliens. But what if the Reds open the box first on one of their settlement worlds?"

There it was again, the old thorn which prodded them into risks and recklessness. Danger ahead on both paths. Don't risk trying to learn galactic secrets, but don't risk your enemy's learning them either. You held a white-hot iron in both hands in this business. And Ashe was right, they had stumbled on something here which hinted that a whole world had been altered to suit some plan. Suppose the secret of that alteration was discovered by their enemies?

"Were the ship and castle people natives?" Ross wondered aloud.

"Just at a guess they were, or at least settlers who had been established here so long they had developed a local form of civilization which was about on the level of a feudal society."

"You mean because of the castle and the rock bombardment. But what about the ships?"

"Two separate phases of a society at war, perhaps a more aggressive against a less technically advanced. American warships paying a visit to the Shogun's Japan, for example."

Ross grinned. "Those warships didn't seem to fancy their welcome. They steered out to sea fast enough when the rocks began to fall."

"Yes, but the ships could exist in the castle pattern; the pylons could not!"

"Which period are you aiming for first—the castle or the pylons?"

"Castle first, I think. Then if we can't pick up any hints, we'll take some jumps forward until we do connect. Only we'll be under severe handicaps. If we could only plant an analyzer somewhere in the castle beginning."

Ross did not show his surprise. If Ashe was talking on those terms, then he was intending to do more than just lurk around a little beyond the gate; he was really planning to pick up alien speech patterns, eventually assume an alien agent identity!

"Gordon!" Karara appeared between two of the lace trees. She came so hastily that the contents of the two cups she carried slopped over. "You must hear what Hori has to say—"

The tall Samoan who trailed her spoke quickly. For the first time since Ross had known him he was very serious, a frown line between his eyes. "There is a bad storm coming. Our instruments register it."

"How long away?" Ashe was on his feet.

"A day . . . maybe two . . ."

Ross could see no change in the sky, islands, or sea. They had had idyllic weather for the six weeks since their planeting, no sign of any such trouble in the Hawaikan paradise.

"It's coming," Hori repeated.

"The gate is half up," Ashe thought aloud, "too much of it set to be dismantled again in a hurry."

"If it's completed," Hori wanted to know, "would it ride out a storm?"

"It might, behind that reef where we have it based. To finish it would be a fast job."

Hori flexed his hands. "We're more brawn than brain in these matters, Gordon, but you've all our help, for what it's worth. What about the ship, does it lift on schedule?"

"Check with Rimbault about that. This storm, how will it compare to a Pacific typhoon?"

The Samoan shook his head. "How do we know? We have not yet had to face the local variety."

"The islands are low," Karara commented. "Winds and water could—"

"Yes! We'd better see Rimbault about a shelter if needed."

If the settlement had drowsed, now its inhabitants were busy. It was decided that they could shelter in the spaceship should the storm reach hurricane proportions, but before its coming the gate must be finished. The final fitting was left to Ashe and Ross, and the older agent fastened the last bolt when the waters beyond the reef were already wind ruffled, the sky darkening fast. The dolphins swam back and forth in the lagoon and with them Karara, though Ashe had twice waved her to the shore.

There was no sunlight left, and they worked with torches. Ashe began his inspection of the relatively simple transfer—the two upright bars, the slab of opaque material forming a doorstep between them. This was only a skeleton of the gates Ross had used in the past. But continual experimentation had produced this more easily transported installation.

Piled in a net were several supply containers ready for an exploring run—extra gill-packs, the analyzer, emergency rations, a medical kit, all the basics. Was Ashe going to try now? He had activated the transfer, the rods were glowing faintly, the slab they guarded having an eerie blue glimmer. He probably only wanted to be sure it worked.

What happened at that moment Ross could never find any adequate words to describe, nor was he sure he could remember. The disorientation of the pass-through he had experienced before; this time he was whirled into a vortex of feeling in which his body, his identity, were rift from him and he lost touch with all stability.

Instinctively he lashed out, his reflexes more than his conscious will keeping him above water in the wild rage of a storm-whipped sea. The light was gone; here was only dark and beating water. Then a lightning flash ripped wide the heavens over Ross as his head broke the surface and he saw, with unbelieving eyes, that he was being thrust shoreward—not to the strand of Finger Island—but against a cliff where water pounded an unyielding wall of rock.

Ross comprehended that somehow he had been jerked through the gate, that he was now fronting the land that had been somewhere beneath the heights supporting the castle. Then he fought for his life to escape the hammer of the sea determined to crack him against the surface of the cliff.

A rough surface loomed up before him, and he threw himself in that direction, embracing a rock, striving to cling through the backwash of the wave which had brought him there. His nails grated and broke on the stone, and then the fingers of his right hand caught in a hole, and he held on with all the strength in his gasping, beaten body. He had had no preparation, no warning, and only the tough survival will which had been trained and bred into him saved his life.

As the water washed back, Ross strove to pull up farther on his anchorage, to be above the strike of the next wave. Somehow he gained a foot before it came. The mask of the gill-pack saved him from being smothered in that curling torrent as he clung stubbornly, resisting again the pull of the retreating sea.

Inch by inch between waves he fought for footing and stable support. Then he was on the surface of the rock, out of all but the lash of spray. He crouched there, spent and gasping. The thunder roar of the surf, and beyond it the deeper mutter of the rage in the heavens, was deafening, dulling his sense as much as the ordeal through which he had passed. He was content to cling where he was, hardly conscious of his surroundings.

Sparks of light along the shore to the north at last caught Ross's attention. They moved, some clustering along the wave line, a few strung up the cliff. And they were not part of the storm's fireworks. Men here—why at this moment?

Another bolt of lightning showed him the answer. On the reef fringe which ran a tongue of land into the sea hung a ship—two ships—pounded by every hammer wave. Shipwrecks . . . and those lights must mark castle dwellers drawn to aid the survivors.

Ross crawled across his rock on his hands and knees, wavered along the cliff wall until he was again faced with angry water. To drop into that would be a mistake. He hesitated—and now more than his own predicament struck home to him.

Ashe, Ashe had been ahead of him at the time gate. If Ross had been jerked through to this past, then somewhere in the water, on the shore, Gordon was here too! But where to find him . . .

Setting his back to the cliff and holding to the rough stone, Ross got to his feet, trying to see through the welter of foam and water. Not only the sea poured here; now a torrential rain fell into the bargain, streaming down about him, battering his head and shoulders. A chill rain which made him shiver.

He wore gill-pack, weighted belt with its sheathed tool and knife, flippers, and the pair of swimming trunks which had been suitable for the Hawaika he knew; but this was a different world altogether. Dare he use his torch to see the way out of here? Ross watched the lights to the north, deciding they were not too unlike his own beam, and took the chance.

Now he stood on a shelf of rock pitted with depressions, all pools. To his left was a drop into a boiling whirling caldron from which points of stone fanged. Ross shuddered. At least he had escaped being pulled into that!

To his right, northward, there was another space of sea, a narrow strip, and then a second ledge. He measured the distance between that and the one on which he perched. Staying where he was would not locate Ashe.

Ross stripped off his flippers, made them fast in his belt. Then he leaped and landed painfully, as his feet slipped and he skidded face down on the northern ledge.

As he sat up, rubbing a bruised and scraped knee, he saw lights advancing in his direction. And between them a shadow crawling from water to shore. Ross stumbled along the ledge hastening to reach that figure, who lay still now just out of the waves. Ashe?

Ross's limping pace became a trot. But he was too late; the other lights, two of them, had reached the shadow. A man—or at least a body which was humanoid—sprawled face down. Other men, three of them, gathered over the exhausted swimmer.

Those who held the torches were still partially in the dark, but the third stooped to roll over their find. Ross caught the glint of light on a metallic headcovering, the glisten of wet armor of some type on the fellow's back and shoulders as he made quick examination of the sea's victim.

Then . . . Ross halted, his eyes wide. A hand rose and fell with expert precision. There had been a blade in that hand. Already the three were turning away from the man so ruthlessly dispatched. Ashe? Or some survivor of the wrecked ships?

Ross retreated to the end of the ledge. The narrow stream of water dividing it from the rock where he had won ashore washed into a cave of the cliff. Dare he try to work his way into that? Masked, with the gill-pack, he could go under surface if he were not smashed by the waves against some wall.

He glanced back. The lights were very close to the end of his ledge. To withdraw to the second rock would mean being caught in a dead end, for he dared not enter the whirlpool on its far side. There was really no choice: stay and be killed, or try for the cave. Ross fastened on his flippers and lowered his body into the narrow stream. The fact that it was narrow and guarded on either side by the ledges tamed the waves a little, and Ross found the tug against him not so great as he feared it would be.

Keeping handholds on the rock, he worked along, head and shoulders often under the wash of rolling water, but winning steadily to the break in the cliff wall. Then he was through, into a space much larger than the opening, water-filled but not with a wild turbulence of waves.

Had he been sighted? Ross kept a handhold to the left of that narrow entrance, his body floating with the rise and fall of the water. He could make out the gleam of light without. It might be that one of those hunters had leaned out over the runnel of the cave entrance, was flashing his torch down into the water there.

Behind mask plate Ross's lips writhed in the snarl of the hunted. In here he would have the advantage. Let one of them, or all three, try to follow through that rock entrance and . . .

But if he had been sighted at the mouth of the lair, none of his trackers appeared to wish to press the hunt. The light disappeared, and Ross was left in the dark. He counted a hundred slowly and then a second hundred before he dared use his own torch.

For all its slit entrance this was a good-sized hideaway he had chanced upon. And he discovered, when he ventured to release his wall hold and swim out into its middle, the bottom arose in a slope toward its rear.

Moments later Ross pulled out of the water once more, to crouch shivering on a ledge only lapped now and then by wavelets. He had found a temporary refuge, but his good fortune did not quiet his fears. Had that been Ashe on the shore? And why had the swimmer been so summarily executed by the men who found him?

The ships caught on the reef, the castle on the cliff above his head . . . enemies . . . ships' crews and castle men? But the callous act of the shore patrol argued a state of war carried to fanatic proportions, perhaps interracial conflict.

He could not hope to explore until the storm was over. To plunge back into the sea would not find Ashe. And to be hunted along the shore by an unknown enemy was simply asking to die without achieving any good in return. No, he must remain where he was for the present.

Ross unhooked the torch from his belt and used it on this higher portion of the cave. He was perched on a ledge which protruded into the water in the form of a wedge. At his back the wall of the cave was rough, and trails of weed were festooned on its projections. The smell of fishy decay was strong enough to register as Ross pulled off his mask. As far as he could now see there was no exit except by sea.

A movement in the water brought his light flashing down into the dark flood. Then a sleek head arose in the path of that ray. Not a man swimming, but one of the dolphins!

Ross's exclamation of surprise was half gasp, half cry. The second dolphin showed for a moment and between a shadow of their bodies, just under the surface, moved a third form.

"Ashe!" Ross had no idea how the dolphins had come through the time gate, but that they had guided to safety a Terran he did not doubt at all. "Ashe!"

But it was not Ashe who came wading to the ledge where Ross waited with hand outstretched. He had been so sure of the other's identity that he blinked in complete bewilderment as his eyes met Karara's and she half stumbled, half reeled against him.

His arms about her shoulders steadied her, and her shivering body was close to his as she leaned her full weight upon him. Her hands made a feeble movement to her mask, and he pulled it off. Uncovered, her face was pale and drawn, her eyes now closed, and her breath came in ragged, tearing sobs which shook her even more.

"How did you get here?" Ross demanded even as he pushed her down on the ledge.

Her head moved slowly, in a weak gesture of negation.

"I don't know . . . we were close to the gate. There was a flash of light . . . then—" Her voice sealed up with a note of hysteria in it. "Then . . . I was here . . . and Taua with me. Tino-rau came . . . Ross, Ross . . . there was a man swimming. He got ashore; he was getting to his feet and—and they killed him!"

Ross's hold tightened; he stared into her face with fierce demand.

"Was it Gordon?"

She blinked, brought her hand up to her mouth, and wiped it back and forth across her chin. There was a small red trickle growing between her fingers, dripping down her arm.

"Gordon?" She repeated it as if she had never heard the name before.

"Yes, did they kill Gordon?"

In his grasp she was swaying back and forth. Then, realizing he was shaking her, Ross got himself under control.

But a measure of understanding had come into her eyes. "No, not Gordon. Where is Gordon?"

"You haven't seen him?" Ross persisted, knowing it was useless.

"Not since we were at the gate." Her words were less slurred. "Weren't you with him?"

"No. I was alone."

"Ross, where are we?"

"Better say—when are we," he replied. "We're through the gate and back in time. And we have to find Gordon!" He did not want to think of what might have happened out on the shore.

## V

## TIME WRECKED

"CAN WE GO BACK?" Karara was herself again, her voice crisp.

"I don't know." Ross gave her the truth. The force which had drawn them through the gate was beyond his experience. As far as he knew, there had never been such an involuntary passage by time gate, and what their trip might mean he did not know.

The main concern was that Ashe must have come through too, and that he was missing. Just let the storm abate, and, with the dolphins' aid, Ross's chance for finding the missing agent was immeasurably better. He said so now, and Karara nodded.

"Do you suppose there is a war going on here?" She hugged her arms across her breast, her shoulders heaving in the torch light with shudders she could not control. The damp chill was biting, and Ross realized that was also danger.

"Could be." He got to his feet, switched the light from the girl to the walls. That seaweed, could it make them some form of protective covering?

"Hold this—aim it there!" He thrust the torch into her hands and went for one of the loops of kelp.

Ross reeled in lines of the stuff. It was rank-smelling but only slightly damp, and he piled it on the ledge in a kind of nest. At least in the hollow of that mound they would be sheltered after a fashion.

Karara crawled into the center of the mass, and Ross followed her. The smell of the stuff filled his nose, was almost like a visible cloud, but he had been right, the girl stopped shivering, and he felt a measure of warmth in his own shaking body. Ross snapped off the torch, and they lay together in the dark, the half-rotten pile of weed holding them.

He must have slept, Ross guessed, when he stirred, raising his head. His body was stiff, aching, as he braced himself up on his hands and peered over the edge of their kelp nest. There was light in the cave, a pale grayish wash which grew stronger toward the slit opening. It must be day. And that meant they could move.

Ross groped in the weed, his hand falling on a curve of shoulder.

"Wake up!" His voice was hoarse and held the snap of an order.

There was a startled gasp in answer, and the mound beside him heaved as the girl stirred.

"Day out—" Ross pointed.

"And the storm—" she stood up, "I think it is over."

It was true that the level of water within the cave had fallen, that wavelets no longer lapped with the same vigor. Morning . . . the storm over . . . and somewhere Ashe!

Ross was about to snap his mask into place when Karara caught at his arm.

"Be careful! Remember what I saw—last night they were killing swimmers!"

He shook her off impatiently. "I'm no fool! And with the packs on we do not have to surface. Listen—" he had another thought, one which would provide an excellent excuse for keeping her safely out of his company, reducing his responsibility for her, "you take the dolphins and try to find the gate. We'll want out as soon as I locate Ashe."

"And if you do not find him soon?"

Ross hesitated. She had not said the rest. What if he could not find Gordon at all? But he would—he had to!

"I'll be back here"—he checked his watch, no longer an accurate timekeeper, for Hawaikan days held an hour more than the Terran twenty-four, but the settlers kept the off-world measurement to check on work periods— "in say, two hours. You should know by then about the gate, and I'll have some idea of the situation along the shore. But listen—" Ross caught her shoulders in a taut grip, pulled her around to face him, his eyes hot and almost angry as they held hers, "don't let yourself be seen—" He repeated the cardinal rule of Agents in new territory. "We don't dare risk discovery."

Karara nodded and he could see that she understood, was aware of the importance of that warning. "Do you want Tino-rau or Taua?"

"No, I'm going to search along the shore first. Ashe would have tried for that last night . . . was probably driven in the way we were. He'd go to ground somewhere. And I have this—" Ross touched the sonic on his belt. "I'll set it on his call; you do the same with yours. Then if we get within distance, he'll pick us up. Back here in two hours—"

"Yes." Karara kicked free of the weed, was already wading down to where the dolphins circled in the cave pool waiting for her. Ross followed, and the four swam for the open sea.

It could not be much after dawn, Ross thought, as he clung by one hand to a rock and watched Karara and the dolphins on their way. Then he paddled along the shore northward for his own survey of the coast. There was a rose cast in the sky, warming the silver along the far reaches of the horizon. And about him bobbed storm flotsam, so that he had to pick a careful way through floating debris.

On the reef one of the wrecked ships had vanished entirely. Perhaps it had been battered to death by the waves, ground to splinters against the rocks. The other still held, its prow well out of the now receding waves, jagged holes in its sides through which spurts of water cascaded now and then.

The wreck which had been driven landward was composed of planks, boxes, and containers rolled by the waves' force. Much of this was already free of the sea, and on the beach figures moved examining it. In spite of the danger of chance discovery, Ross edged along rocks, seeking a vantage point from which he could watch that activity.

He was flat against a sea-girt boulder, a swell of floating weed draped about him, when the nearest of the foraging parties moved into good view.

Men . . . at least they had the outward appearance of men much like himself, though their skin was dark and their limbs appeared disproportionately long and thin. There were two groups of them, four wearing only a scanty loincloth, busy turning over and hunting through the debris under the direction of the other two.

The workers had thick growths of hair which not only covered their heads, but down their spines and the outer sides of their thin arms and legs to elbow and knee. The hair was a pallid yellow-white in vivid contrast to their dark skins, and their chins protruded sharply, allowing the lower line of their faces to take on a vaguely disturbing likeness to an animal's muzzle.

Their overseers were more fully clothed, wearing not only helmets on their heads, whose helms had a protective visor over the face, but also breast- and backplates molded to their bodies. Ross thought that these could not be solid metal since they adapted to the movements of the wearers.

Feet and legs were covered with casing combinations of shoe and leggings, colored dull red. They were armed with swords of an odd pattern; their points curved up so that the blade resembled a fishhook. Unsheathed, the blades were clipped to a waist belt by catches which glittered in the weak morning light as if gem set.

Ross could see little of their faces, for the beak visors overhung their features. But their skins were as dusky as those of the laborers, and their arms and legs of the same unusual length . . . men of the same race, he deduced.

Under the orders of the armed overseers the laborers were reducing the beach to order, sorting out the flotsam into two piles. Once they gathered about a find, and the sound of excited speech reached Ross as an agitated clicking. The armored men came up, surveyed the discovery. One of them shrugged, and clicked an order.

Ross caught only a half glimpse of the thing two of the workers dragged away. A body! Ashe . . . The Terran was about to move closer when he saw the green cloak dragging about the corpse. No, not Gordon, just another victim from the wrecks.

The aliens were working their way toward Ross, and perhaps it was time for him to go. He was pushing aside his well-arranged curtain of weed when he was startled by a shout. For a second he thought he might have been sighted, until resulting action on shore told him otherwise.

The furred workers shrank back against the mound to which they had just dragged the body. While the two guards took up a position before them, curved swords, snapped from their belt hooks, ready in their hands. Again that shout. Was it a warning or a threat? With the language barrier Ross could only wait to see.

Another party approached along the beach from the south. In the load was a cloaked and hooded figure, so muffled in its covering of silver-gray that Ross had no idea of the form beneath. Silver-gray—no, now that hue was deepening with blue tones, darkening rapidly. By the time the cloaked newcomer had passed the rock which sheltered the Terran the covering was a rich blue which seemed to glow.

Behind the leader were a dozen armed men. They wore the same beaked helmets, the supple encasing breast- and back-plates, but their leggings were gray. They, too, carried curved swords, but the weapons were still latched to their belts and they made no move to draw them in spite of the very patent hostility of the guards before them.

Blue cloak halted some three feet from the guards. The sea wind pulled at the cloak, wrapping it about the body beneath. But even so, the wearer remained well hidden. From under a flapping edge came a hand. The fingers, long and slender, were curled about an ivory-colored wand which ended in a knob. Sparks flashed from it in a continuous flickering.

Ross clapped his hand to his belt. To his complete amazement the sonic disk he wore was reacting to those flashes, prickling sharply in perfect beat to their blink-blink. The Terran cupped his scarred fingers over the disk as he waited to see what was going to happen, wondering if the holder of that wand might, in return, pick up the broadcast of the code set on Ashe's call.

The hand holding the wand was not dusky-skinned but had much of the same ivory shade as the rod, so that to Ross the meeting between flesh and wand was hardly distinguishable. Now by one firm thrust the hand planted the rod into the sand, leaving it to stand sentinel between the two parties.

Retreating a step or two, the red-clad guards gave ground. But they did not reclasp their swords. Their attitude, Ross judged, was that of men in some awe of their opponent, but men urged to defiance, either by a belief in the righteousness of their cause, or strengthened by an old hatred.

Now the cloaked one began to speak—or was that speech? Certainly the flow of sound had little in common with the clicking tongue Ross had caught earlier. This trill of notes possessed the rise and fall of a chant or song which could have been a formula of greeting—or a warning. And the lines of warriors escorting the chanter stood to attention, their weapons still undrawn.

Ross caught his lower lip between his teeth and bit down on it. That chanting—it crawled into the mind, set up a pattern! He shook his head vigorously and then was shocked by that recklessness. Not that any of those on shore had glanced in his direction.

The chant ended on a high, broken note. It was followed by a moment of silence through which sounded only the wind and the beat of wave.

Then one of the laborers flung up his head and clicked a word or two. He and his fellows fell face down on the beach, cupping their hands to pour sand over their unkempt heads. One of the guards turned with a sharp yell to boot the nearest of the workers in the ribs.

But his companion cried out. The wand which had stood so erect when it was first planted, now inclined toward the working party, its sparks shooting so swiftly and with such slight break between that they were fast making a single beam. Ross jerked his hand from contact with the sonic; a distinct throb of pain answered that stepping up of the mysterious broadcast.

The laborers broke and ran, or rather crawled on their bellies until they were well away, before they got to their feet and pelted back down the strand. However, the guards were of sterner stuff. They were withdrawing all right, but slowly backing away, their swords held up before them as men might retreat before insurmountable odds.

When they were well gone the robed one took up the wand. Holding it out beyond, the cloaked leader of the second party approached the two piles of salvage the workers had heaped into rough order. There was a detailed inspection of both until the robed one came upon the body.

At a trilled order two of the warriors came up and laid out the corpse. When the robed one nodded they stood well back. The rod moved, the tip rather than the knobbed head being pointed at the body.

Ross's head snapped back. That bolt of light, energy, fire—whatever it was—issuing from the rod had dazzled him into momentary blindness. And a vibration of force through the air was like a blow.

When he was able to see once more there was nothing at all on the sand where the corpse had lain, nothing except a glassy trough from which some spirals of vapor arose. Ross clung to his rock support badly shaken.

Men with swords . . . and now this—some form of controlled energy which argued of technical development and science. Just as the cliff castle had bombarded with rocks ships sailing with a speed which argued engine power of an unknown type. A mixture of barbaric and advanced knowledge. To assess this, he needed more experience, more knowledge than he possessed. Now Ashe could . . .

Ashe!

Ross was jerked back to his own quest. The rod was quiet, no more sparks were flung from its knob. And under Ross's touch his sonic was quiet also. He snapped off the broadcast. If that device had picked up the flickering of the rod, the reverse could well be true.

The cloaked one chose from the pile of goods, and its escort gathered up the designated boxes, a small cask or two. So laden, the party returned south the way they had come. Ross allowed his breath to expel in a sigh of relief.

He worked his way farther north along the coast, watching other parties of the furred workers and their guards. Lines of the former climbed the cliff, hauling their spoil, their destination the castle. But Ross saw no sign of Ashe, received no answer to the sonic code he had reset once the strangers were out of distance. And the Terran began to realize that his present search might well be fruitless, though he fought against accepting it.

When he turned back to the slit cave Ross's fear was ready to be expressed in anger, the anger of frustration over his own helplessness. With no chance of trying to penetrate the castle, he could not learn whether or not Ashe had been taken prisoner. And until the workers left the beach he could not prowl there hunting the grimmer evidence his mind flinched from considering.

Karara waited for him on the inner ledge. There was no sign of the dolphins and as Ross pulled out of the water, pushing aside his mask, her face in the thin light of the cave was deeply troubled.

"You did not find him," she made that a statement rather than a question.

"No."

"And I did not find it—"

Ross used a length of weed from the nest as a towel. But now he stood very still.

"The gate . . . no sign of it?"

"Just this—" She reached behind her and brought up a sealed container. Ross recognized one of the supply cans they had had in the cache by the gate. "There are others . . . scattered. Taua and Tino-rau seek them now. It is as if all that was on the other side was sucked through with us."

"You are sure you found the right place?"

"Is—is this not part of it?" Again the girl sought for something on the ledge. What she held out to him was a length of metal rod, twisted and broken at one end as if a giant hand had wrenched it loose from the installation.

Ross nodded dully. "Yes," his voice was harsh as if the words were pulled out of him against his will and against all hope—"that's part of a side bar. It—it must have been totally wrecked."

Yet, even though he held that broken length in his hands, Ross could not really believe the gate was gone. He swam out once more, heading for the reef where the dolphins joined him as guides. There was a second piece of broken tube, the scattered containers of supplies, that was all. The Terrans were wrecked in time as surely as those ships had been wrecked on the sea reef the night before!

Ross headed once again for the cave. Their immediate

needs were of major importance now. The containers must be all gathered and taken into their hiding place, because upon their contents three human lives could depend.

He paused just at the entrance to adjust the net of containers he transported. And it was that slight chance which brought him knowledge of the intruder.

On the ledge Karara was heaping up the kelp of the nest. But to one side and on a level with the girl's head . . .

Ross dared not flash his torch, thus betraying his presence. Leaving the net hitched to the rock by its sling, he swam under water along the side of the cave by a route which should bring him out within striking distance of that hunched figure perching above to watch Karara's every move.

## VI

## LOKETH THE USELESS

THE WASH of waves covered Ross's advance until he came up against the wall not too far from the spy's perch. Whoever crouched there still leaned forward to watch Karara. And Ross's eyes, having adjusted to the gloom of the cavern, made out the outline of head and shoulders. The next two or three minutes were the critical ones for the Terran. He must emerge on the ledge in the open before he could attack.

Karara might almost have read his mind and given conscious help. For now she went out on the point of the ledge to whistle the dolphin's summons. Tino-rau's sleek head bobbed above water as he answered the girl with a bubbling squeak. Karara knelt and the dolphin came to butt against her outheld hand.

Ross heard a gasp from the watcher, a faint sound of movement. Karara began to sing softly, her voice rippling in one of the liquid chants of her own people, the dolphin interjecting a note or two. Ross had heard them at that before, and it made perfect cover for his move. He sprang.

His grasp tightened on flesh, fingers closed about thin wrists. There was a yell of astonishment and fear from the stranger as the Terran jerked him from his perch to the ledge. Ross had his opponent flattened under him before he realized that the other had offered no struggle, but lay still.

"What is it?" Karara's torch beam caught them both. Ross looked down into a thin brown face not too different from his own. The wide-set eyes were closed, and the mouth gaped open. Though he believed the Hawaikan unconscious, Ross still kept hold on those wrists as he moved from the sprawled body. With the girl's aid he used a length of kelp to secure the captive.

The stranger wore a garment of glistening skintight material which covered body, legs, and feet, but left his lanky arms bare. A belt about his waist had loops for a number of objects, among them a hook-pointed knife which Ross prudently removed.

"Why, he is only a boy," Karara said. "Where did he come from, Ross?"

The Terran pointed to the wall crevice. "He was up there, watching you."

Her eyes were wide and round. "Why?"

Ross dragged his prisoner back against the wall of the cave. After witnessing the fate of those who had swum ashore from the wreck, he did not like to think what motive might have brought the Hawaikan here. Again Karara's thoughts must have matched his, for she added:

"But he did not even draw his knife. What are you going to do with him, Ross?"

That problem already occupied the Terran. The wisest move undoubtedly was to kill the native out of hand. But such ruthlessness was more than he could stomach. And if he could learn anything from the stranger—gain some knowledge of this new world and its ways—he would be twice winner. Why, this encounter might even lead to Ashe!

"Ross . . . his leg. See?" The girl pointed.

The tight fit of the alien's clothing made the defect clear; the right leg of the stranger was shrunken and twisted. He was a cripple.

"What of it?" Ross demanded sharply. This was no time for an appeal to the sympathies.

But Karara did not urge any modification of the bonds as he half feared she would. Instead, she sat back cross-legged, an odd, withdrawn expression making her seem remote though he could have put out his hand to touch her.

"His lameness—it could be a bridge," she observed, to Ross's mystification.

"A bridge—what do you mean?"

The girl shook her head. "This is only a feeling, not a true thought. But also it is important. Look, I think he is waking."

The lids above those large eyes were fluttering. Then with a shake of the head, the Hawaikan blinked up at them. Blank bewilderment was all Ross could read in the stranger's expression until the alien saw Karara. Then a flood of clicking speech poured from his lips.

He seemed utterly astounded when they made no answer. And the fluency of his first outburst took on a pleading note, while the expectancy of his first greeting faded away.

Karara spoke to Ross. "He is becoming afraid, very much afraid. At first, I think, he was pleased . . . happy."

"But why?"

The girl shook her head. "I do not know: I can only feel. Wait!" Her hand rose in imperious command. She did not rise to her feet, but crawled on hands and knees to the edge of the ledge. Both dolphins were there, raising their heads well out of the water, their actions expressing unusual excitement.

"Ross!" Karara's voice rang loudly. "Ross, they can understand him! Tino-rau and Taua can understand him!"

"You mean, they understand this language?" Ross found that fantastic, awesome as the abilities of the dolphins were.

"No, his mind. It's his mind, Ross. Somehow he thinks in patterns they can pick up and read! They do that, you know, with a few of us, but not in the same way. This is more direct, clearer! They're so excited!"

Ross glanced at the prisoner. The alien had wriggled

about, striving to raise his head against the wall as a support. His captor pulled the Hawaikan into a sitting position, but the native accepted that aid almost as if he were not even aware of Ross's hands on his body. He stared with a kind of horrified disbelief at the bobbing dolphin heads.

"He is afraid," Karara reported. "He has never known such communication before."

"Can they ask him questions?" demanded Ross. If this odd mental tie between Terran dolphin and Hawaikan did exist, then there was a chance to learn about this world.

"They can try. Now he only knows fear, and they must break through that."

What followed was the most unusual four-sided conversation Ross could have ever imagined. He put a question to Karara, who relayed it to the dolphins. In turn, they asked it mentally of the Hawaikan and conveyed his answer back via the same route.

It took some time to allay the fears of the stranger. But at last the Hawaikan entered wholeheartedly into the exchange.

"He is the son of the lord ruling the castle above." Karara produced the first rational and complete answer. "But for some reason he is not accepted by his own kind. Perhaps," she added on her own, "it is because he is crippled. The sea is his home, as he expresses it, and he believes me to be some mythical being out of it. He saw me swimming masked, and with the dolphins, and he is sure I change shape at will."

She hesitated. "Ross, I get something odd here. He does know, or thinks he knows, creatures who can appear and disappear at will. And he is afraid of their powers."

"Gods and goddesses—perfectly natural."

Karara shook her head. "No, this is more concrete than a religious belief."

Ross had a sudden inspiration. Hurriedly he described

the cloaked figure who had driven the castle people from the piles of salvage. "Ask him about that one."

She relayed the question. Ross saw the prisoner's head jerk around. The Hawaikan looked from Karara to her companion, a shade of speculation in his expression.

"He wants to know why you ask about the Foanna? Surely you must well know what manner of beings they are."

"Listen—" Ross was sure now that he had made a real discovery, though its importance he could not guess, "tell him we come from where there are no Foanna. That we have powers and must know of their powers."

If he could only carry on this interrogation straight and not have to depend upon a double translation! And could he even be sure his questions reached the alien undistorted?

Wearily Ross sat back on his heels. Then he glanced at Karara with a twinge of concern. If he was tired by their roundabout communication, she must be doubly so. There was a droop to her shoulders, and her last reply had come in a voice hoarse with fatigue. Abruptly he started up.

"That's enough—for now."

Which was true. He had to have time for evaluation, to adjust to what they had learned during the steady stream of questions passed back and forth. And in that moment he was conscious of his hunger, just as his voice was paper dry from lack of drink. The canister of supplies he had left by the cave entrance . . .

"We need food and drink." He fumbled with his mask, but Karara motioned him back from the water.

"Taua brings . . . Wait!"

The dolphin trailed the net of containers to them. Ross unscrewed one, pulled out a bulb of fresh water. A second box yielded the dry wafers of emergency rations.

Then, after a moment's hesitation, Ross crossed to the prisoner, cut his wrist bonds, and pressed both a bulb and a wafer into his hold. The Hawaikan watched the Terrans eat before he bit into the wafer, chewing it with vigor, turning the bulb around in his fingers with alert interest before he sucked at its contents.

As Ross chewed and swallowed, mechanically and certainly with no relish, he fitted one fact to another to make a picture of this Hawaikan time period in which they were now marooned. Of course, his picture was based on facts they had learned from their captive. Perhaps he had purposely misled them or fogged some essentials. But could he have done that in a mental contact? Ross would simply have to accept everything with a certain amount of cautious skepticism.

Anyway, there were the Wreckers of the castle—petty lordlings setting up their holds along the coasts, preying upon the shipping which was the lifeblood of this island-water world. The Terrans had seen them in action last night and today. And if the captive's information was correct, it was not only the storm's fury which brought the wave's harvest. The Wreckers had some method of attracting ships to crack up on their reefs.

Some method of attraction . . . And that force which had pulled the Terrans through the time gate; could there be a connection? However, there remained the Wreckers on the cliff. And their prey, the seafarers of the ocean, with an understandably deep enmity between them.

Those two parties Ross could understand and be prepared to deal with, he thought. But there remained the Foanna. And from their prisoner's explanation, the Foanna were a very different matter.

They possessed a power which did not depend upon swords or ships or the natural tools and weapons of men. No, they had strengths which were unearthly, to give them superiority in all but one way—numbers. Though the Foanna had their warriors and servants, as Ross had seen on the beach, they, themselves, were of another race—a very old and dying race of which few remained. How many, their enemies could not say, for the Foanna had no separate identities known to the outer world. They appeared, gave their orders, levied their demands, opposed or aided as they wished—always just one or two at a time—always so muffled in their cloaks that even their physical appearances remained a mystery. But there was no mystery about their powers. Ross gathered that no Wrecker lord, no matter how much a leader among his own kind, how ambitious, had yet dared to oppose actively one of the Foanna, though he might make a token protest against some demand from them.

And certainly the captive's description of those powers in action suggested a supernatural origin of Foanna knowledge, or at least for its application. But Ross thought that the answer might be that they possessed the remnants of some almost forgotten technical know-how, the heritage of a very old race. He had tried to learn something of the origin of the Foanna themselves, wondering if the robed ones could be from the galactic empire. But the answer had come that the Foanna were older than recorded time, that they had lived in the great citadel before the race of the Terrans' prisoner had risen from very primitive savagery.

"What-do we do now?" Karara broke in upon Ross's thoughts as she refastened the containers.

"These slaves that the Wreckers take upon occasion . . . Maybe Ashe . . ." Ross was catching at very fragile straws; he had to. And the stranger had said that able-bodied men who swam ashore relatively uninjured were taken captive. Several had been the night before.

"Loketh."

Ross and Karara looked around. The prisoner put down the water bulb, and one of his hands made a gesture they could not mistake; he pointed to himself and repeated that word, "Loketh."

The Terran touched his own chest. "Ross Murdock."

Perhaps the other was as impatient as he with their

round-about method of communication and had decided to try and speed it up. The analyzer! Ashe had included the analyzer with the equipment by the gate. If Ross could find that . . . why, then the major problem could be behind them. Swiftly he explained to Karara, and with a vigorous nod of assent she called to Taua, ordering the rest of the salvage material from the gate be brought to them.

"Loketh." Ross pointed to the youth. "Ross." That was himself. "Karara." He indicated the girl.

"Rosss." The alien made a clicking hiss of the first name. "Karara—" He did better with the second.

Ross carefully unpacked the box Taua had located. He had only slight knowledge of how the device worked. It was intended to record a strange language, break it down into symbols already familiar to the Time Agents. But could it also be used as a translator with a totally alien tongue? He could only hope that the rough handling of its journey through the gate had not damaged it and that the experiment might possibly work.

Putting the box between them, he explained what he wanted; and Karara took up the small micro-disk, speaking slowly and distinctly the same liquid syllables she had used in the dolphin song. Ross clicked the lever when she was finished, and watched the small screen. The symbols which flashed there had meaning for him right enough; he could translate what she had just taped. The machine still worked to that extent.

Now he pushed the box into place before Loketh and made the visibly reluctant Hawaikan take the disk from Karara. Then through the dolphin link Ross passed on definite instructions. Would it work as well to translate a stellar tongue as it had with languages past and present of his own planet?

Reluctantly Loketh began to talk to the disk, at first in a very rapid mumble and then, as there was no frightening response, with less speed and more confidence. There were symbol lines on the vista-plate in accordance, and some of them made sense! Ross was elated.

"Ask him: Can one enter the castle unseen to check on the slaves?"

"For what reason?"

Ross was sure he had read those symbols correctly.

"Tell him—that one of our kind may be among them."

Loketh did not reply so quickly this time. His eyes, grave and measuring, studied Ross, then Karara, then Ross again.

"There is a way . . . discovered by this useless one."

Ross did not pay attention to the odd adjective Loketh chose to describe himself. He pressed to the important matter.

"Can and will he show me that way?"

Again that long moment of appraisal on the part of Loketh, before he answered. Ross found himself reading the reply symbols aloud.

"If you dare, then I will lead."

## VII

## WITCHES' MEAT

HE MIGHT be recklessly endangering all of them, Ross knew. But if Ashe was immured somewhere in that rock pile over their heads, then the risk of trusting Loketh would be worth it. However, because Ross was chancing his own neck did not mean that Karara need be drawn into immediate peril too. With the dolphins at her command and the supplies, scanty as those were, she would have a good chance to hide here safely.

"Holding out for what?" she asked quietly after Ross elaborated on this subject, thus bringing him to silence.

Because her question was just. With the gate gone the Terrans were committed to this time, just as they had earlier been committed to Hawaika when on their home world they had entered the spaceship for the take-off. There was no escape from the past, which had become their present.

"The Foanna," she continued, "these Wreckers, the sea people—all at odds with one another. Do we join any, then their quarrels must also be ours."

Taua nosed the ledge behind the girl, squeaked a demand for attention. Karara looked around at Loketh; her look was as searching as the one the native had earlier turned on her and Ross.

"He"—the girl nodded at the Hawaikan—"wishes to know if you trust him. And he says to tell you this: Because the Shades chose to inflict upon him a twisted leg he is not one with those of the castle, but to them a broken, useless thing. Ross, I gather he thinks we have powers like the Foanna, and that we may be super-

thick it fell in tangible folds about his sweating body. Ross almost cried out as fingers clamped about his wrist when he reached for a new hold. Then urged by that grasp, he was up and out, sprawling into a vertical passage. Far ahead was a gray of faint light.

Ross choked and then sneezed as dust puffed up from between his scrabbling hands. The hold which had been on his wrist shifted to his shoulder, and with a surprising strength Loketh hauled the Terran to his feet.

The passage in which they stood was a slit extending in height well above their heads, but narrow, not much wider than Ross's shoulders. Whether it was a natural fault or had been cut he could not tell.

Loketh was ahead again, his rocking limp making the outline of his body a jerky up-and-down shadow. Again his speed and agility amazed the Terran. Loketh might be lame, but he had learned to adapt to his handicap very well.

The light increased and Ross marked slits in the walls to his right, no wider than the breadth of his two fingers. He peered out of one and was looking into empty air while below he heard the murmur of the sea. This way must run in the cliff face above the beach.

A click of impatient whisper drew him on to join Loketh. Here was a flight of stairs, narrow of tread and very steep. Loketh turned back and side against these to climb, his outspread hand flattened on the stone as if it possessed adhesive qualities to steady him. For the first time his twisted leg was a disadvantage.

Ross counted again—ten, fifteen of those steps, bringing them once more into darkness. Then they emerged from a well-like opening into a circular room. A sudden and dazzling flare of light made the Terran shade his eyes. Loketh set a pallid but glowing cone on a wall shelf, and the Terran discovered that the burst of light was only relative to the dark of the passage; indeed it was very weak illumination.

The Hawaikan braced his body against the far wall.

The strain of his effort, whatever its purpose, was easy to read in the controlled line of his shoulders. Then the wall slid under Loketh's urging, a slow move as if the weight of the slab he strove to handle was almost too great for his slender arms, or else the need for caution was intensified here.

They now fronted a narrow opening, and the light of the cone shone only a few feet into the space. Loketh beckoned to Ross and they went on. Here the left wall was cut in many places emitting patches of light in a way which bore no resemblance to conventional windows. It was like walking behind a pierced screen which followed no logical pattern in the cutaway portions. Ross gazed out and gasped.

He was standing above the center core of the castle, and the life below and beyond drew his attention. He had seen drawings reproducing the life of a feudal castle. This resembled them and yet, as Ross studied the scene closer, the differences between the Terran past and this became more distinct.

In the first place there were those animals—or were they animals?—being hooked up to a cart. They had six limbs, walking on four, holding the remaining two folded under their necks. Their harness consisted of a network fitted over their shoulders, anchored to the folded limbs. Their grotesque heads, bobbing and weaving on lengthy necks, their bodies, were sleekly scaled. Ross was startled by a resemblance he traced to the sea dragon he had met in the future of this world.

But the creatures were subject to the men harnessing them. And the activity in other respects . . . Ross had to fight a wayward and fascinated interest in all he could see, force himself to concentrate on learning what might be pertinent to his own mission. But Loketh did not allow him to watch for long. Instead, his hand on the Terran's arm urged the other down the gallery behind the screen and once more into the bulk of the fortress.

Another narrow way ran through the thickness of the

walls. Then a patch of light, not that of outer day, but a reddish gleam from an opening waist high. There Loketh went awkwardly to his good knee, motioning Ross to follow his example.

What lay below was a hall furnished with a barbaric rawness of color and glitter. There were long strips of brightly hued woven stuff on the walls, touched here and there with sparkling glints which were jewel-like. And set at intervals among the hangings were oval objects perhaps Ross's height on which were designs and patterns picked out in paint and metal. Maybe the stylized representation of native plants and animals.

The whole gave an impression of clashing color, just as the garments of those gathered there were garish in turn.

There were three Hawaikans on the two-step dais. All wore robes fitting tightly to the upper portion of their bodies, girded to their waists with elaborate belts, then falling in long points to floor level, the points being finished off with tassels. Their heads were covered with tight caps which were a latticework of decorated strips, glittering as they moved. And the mixture of colors in their apparel was such as to offend Terran eyes with their harsh clash of shade against shade.

Drawn up below the dais were two rows of guards. But the reason for the assembly baffled Ross, since he could not understand the clicking speech.

There came a hollow echoing sound as from a gong. The three on the dais straightened, turning their attention to the other end of the hall. Ross did not need Loketh's gesture to know that something of importance was about to begin.

Down the hall was a somber note in the splash of clashing color. The Terran recognized the gray-blue robe of the Foanna. There were three of the robed ones this time, one slightly in advance of the other two. They came at a gliding pace as if they swept along above that paved flooring, not by planting feet upon it. As they halted below the dais the men there rose.

Ross could read their reluctance to make that concession in the slowness of their movements. They were plainly being compelled to render deference when they longed to refuse it. Then the middle one of the castle lords spoke first.

"Zahur—" Loketh, breathed in Ross's ear, his pointed finger indicating the speaker.

Ross longed vainly for the ability to ask questions, a chance to know what was in progress. That the meeting of the two Hawaikan factions was important he did not doubt.

There was an interval of silence after the castle lord finished speaking. To the Terran this spun on and on and he sensed the mounting tension. This must be a showdown, perhaps even a declaration of open hostilities between Wreckers and the older race. Or perhaps the pause was a subtle weapon of the Foanna, used to throw a less-sophisticated enemy off balance, as a judo fighter might use an opponent's attack as part of his own defense.

When the Foanna did make answer it came in the sing-song of chanted words. Ross felt Loketh shiver, felt the crawl of chill along his own spine. The words—if those were words and not just sounds intended to play upon the mind and emotions of a listener—cut into one. Ross wanted to close his ears, thrust his fingers into them to drown out that sound, yet he did not have the power to raise his hands.

It seemed to him that the men on the dais were swaying now as if the chant were a rope leashed about them, pulling them back and forth. There was a clatter; one of the guards had fallen to the floor and lay there, rolling, his hands to his head.

A shout from the dais. The chanting reached a note so high that Ross felt the torment in his ears. Below, the lines of guards had broken. A party of them were heading for the end of the hall, making a wide detour around the Foanna. Loketh gave a small choked cry; his fingers tightened on Ross's forearm with painful intensity as he whispered.

What was about to happen meant something important. To Loketh or to him? Ashe! Was this concerned with Ashe? Ross crowded against the opening, tried to see the direction in which the guards had disappeared.

The wait made him doubly impatient. One of the men on the dais had dropped on the bench there, his head forward on his hands, his shoulders quivering. But the one Loketh had identified as Zahur still fronted the Foanna spokesman, and Ross gave tribute to the strength of will which kept him there.

They were returning, the guards, and herded between their lines three men. Two were Hawaikans, their bare dark bodies easily identifiable. But the third—Ashe! Ross almost shouted his name aloud.

The Terran stumbled along and there was a bandage above his knee. He had been stripped to his swimming trunks, all his equipment taken from him. There was a dark bruise on his left temple, the angry weal of a lash mark on neck and shoulder.

Ross's hands clenched. Never in his life had he so desperately wanted a weapon as he did at that moment. To spray the company below with a machine gun would have given him great satisfaction. But he had nothing but the knife in his belt and he was as cut off from Ashe as if they were in separate cells of some prison.

The caution which had been one of his inborn gifts and which had been fostered by his training, clamped down on his first wild desire for action. There was not the slightest chance of his doing Ashe any good at the present. But he had this much—he knew that Gordon was alive and that he was in the aliens' hands. Faced by those facts Ross could plan his own moves.

The Foanna chant began again, and the three prisoners moved; the two Hawaikans turned, set themselves on either side of Ashe, and gave him support. Their actions had a mechanical quality as if they were directed by a will beyond their own. Ashe gazed about him at the Wreckers and the robed figures. His awareness of them both suggested to Ross that if the natives had come under the control of the Foanna, the Terran resisted their influence. But Ashe did not try to escape the assistance of his two fellow prisoners, and he limped with their aid back down the hall, following the Foanna.

Ross deduced that the captives had been transferred from the lord of the castle to the Foanna. Which meant Ashe was on his way to another destination. The Terran was on his feet and headed back, intent on returning to the sea cave and starting out after Ashe as soon as he could.

"You have found Gordon!" Karara read his news from his face.

"The Wreckers had him prisoner. Now they've turned him over to the Foanna—"

"What will *they* do with him?" the girl demanded of Loketh.

His answer came roundabout as usual as the native squatted by the analyzer and clicked his answer into it.

"They have claimed the wreck survivors for tribute. Your companion will be witches' meat."

"Witches' meat?" repeated Ross, uncomprehending.

Then Karara drew a gagged breath which was a gasp of horror.

"Sacrifice! Ross, he must mean they are going to use Gordon for a sacrifice."

Ross stiffened and then whirled to catch Loketh by the shoulders. The inability to question the native directly was an added disaster now.

"Where are they taking him? Where?" He began that fiercely, and then forced control on himself.

Karara's eyes were half closed, her head back; she was manifestly aiming that inquiry at the dolphins, to be transmitted to Loketh.

Symbols burned on the analyzer screen.

"The Foanna have their own fortress. It can be entered best by sea. There is a boat . . . I can show you, for it is my own secret."

"Tell him—yes, as soon as we can!" Ross broke out. The old feeling that time was all-important worried at him. Witches' meat . . . witches' meat . . . the words were sharp as a lash.

## VIII

## THE FREE ROVERS

TWILIGHT MADE a gray world where one could not trace the true meeting of land and water, sea and sky. Surely the haze about them was more than just the normal dusk of coming night.

Ross balanced in the middle of the skiff as it bobbed along the swell of waves inside a barrier reef. To his mind the craft carrying the three of them and their net of supplies was too frail, rode too high. But Karara paddling in the bow, Loketh at the stern seemed to be content, and Ross could not, for pride's sake, question their competence. He comforted himself with the knowledge that no agent was able to absorb every primitive skill, and Karara's people had explored the Pacific in outrigger canoes hardly more stable than their present vessel, navigating by currents and stars.

Smothering his feeling of helplessness and the slow anger that roused in him, the Terran busied himself with study of a sort. They had had the longer part of the day in the cave before Loketh would agree to venture out of hiding and paddle south. Ross, using the analyzer, had, with Loketh's aid, set about learning what he could of the native tongue.

Now possessed of a working vocabulary of clicked words, he was able to follow Loketh's speech so that translation through the dolphins was not necessary except for complicated directions. Also, he had a more detailed briefing of the present situation on Hawaika.

Enough to know that they might be embarking on a mad venture. The citadel of the Foanna was distinctly forbidden ground, not only for Loketh's people but also for the Foanna's Hawaikan followers who were housed and labored in an outer ring of fortification-cum-village. Those natives were, Ross gathered, a hereditary corps of servants and warriors, born to that status and not recruited from the native population at large. As such, they were armored by the "magic" of their masters.

"If the Foanna are so powerful," Ross had demanded, "why do you go with us against them?" To depend so heavily on the native made him uneasy.

The Hawaikan looked to Karara. One of his hands raised; his fingers sketched a sign toward the girl.

"With the Sea Maid and her magic I do not fear." He paused before adding, "Always has it been said of me—and to me—that I am a useless one, fit only to do women's tasks. No word weaver shall ever chant my battle deeds in the great hall of Zahur. I who am Zahur's true son can not carry my sword in any lord's train. But now you offer me one of the great-to-be-remembered quests. If I go, so may I prove that I am a man, even if I go limpingly. There is nothing the Foanna can do to me which is worse than what the Shadow has already done. Choosing to follow you I may stand up to face Zahur in his own hall, show him that the blood of his House has not been drained from my veins because I walk crookedly!"

There was such bitter fire, not only in the sputtering rush of Loketh's words, but in his eyes, his face, the wry twist of his lips, that Ross believed him. The Terran no longer had any doubts that the castle outcast was willing to brave the unknown terrors of the Foanna keep, not just to aid Ross whom he considered himself bound to serve by the customs of his people, but because he saw in this venture a chance to gain what he had never had, a place in his warrior culture.

Shut off from the normal life of his people, he had early turned to the sea. His twisted leg had not proved a handicap in the water, and he stated with confidence that he was the best swimmer in the castle. Not that the men of his father's following had taken greatly to the sea, which they looked upon merely as a way of preying upon the true sea rovers.

The reef on which the ships had been wrecked was a snare of sorts—first by the whim of nature when wind and current piled up the trading ships there. Then, Ross was startled when Loketh elaborated on a later development of that trap.

"So Zahur returned from this meeting and set up a great magic among the rocks, according to the spells he was taught. Now ships are drawn there so the wrecks have been many and Zahur becomes an even greater lord with many men coming to take sword oath under him."

"This magic," asked Ross, "of what manner is it and where did Zahur obtain it?"

"It is fashioned so—" Loketh sketched two straight lines in the air, "not curved as a sword. And the color of water under a storm sky, both rods being as tall as a man. There was much care to set them in place, that was done by a man of Glicmas."

"A man of Glicmas?"

"Glicmas is now the high lord of the Iccio. He is blood kin to Zahur, yet Zahur must take sword oath to send to Glicmas a fourth of all his sea-gleanings for a year in payment for this magic."

"And Glicmas, where did he get it? From the Foanna?"

Loketh made an emphatic denial of that. "No, the Foanna have spoken out against their use, making even greater ill feeling between the Old Ones and the coast people. It is said that Glicmas saw a great wonder in the sky and followed it to a high place of his own country. A mountain broke in twain and a voice issued forth from the rent, calling that the lord of the country come and stand to hear it. When Glicmas did so he was told that the magic would be his. Then the mountain closed again and he found many strange things upon the ground. As he uses them they make him akin to the Foanna in power. Some he gives to those who are his blood kin, and together they will be great until they close their fists not only upon the sea rovers, but upon the Foanna also. This they have come to believe."

"But you do not?" Karara asked then.

"I do not know, Sea Maid. The time is coming when perhaps they shall have their chance to prove how strong is their magic. Already the Rovers gather in fleets as they never did before. And it seems that they, too, have found a new magic, for their ships fly through the water, depending no longer on wind-filling sails, or upon strong arms of men at long paddles. There is a struggle before us. But that you must know, being who and what you are, Sea Maid."

"And what do you think I am? What do you think Ross is?"

"If the Foanna dwell on land and hold old knowledge and power beyond our reckoning in their two hands," he replied, "then it is possible that the same could have roots in the sea. It is my belief that you are of the Shades, but not the Shadow. And this warrior is also of your kind—but perhaps in different degree, putting into action your desires and wishes. Thus, if you go up against the Foanna, you shall be well matched, kind to kind."

Nice to be so certain of that, Ross thought. He did not share Loketh's confidence on that subject.

"The Shades . . . the Shadow . . ." Karara persisted. "What are these, Loketh?"

An odd expression crossed the Hawaikan's face. "Are those not known to you, Sea Maid? Indeed, then you are of a breed different from the men of land. The Shades are those of power who may come to the aid of men should it be their desire to influence the future. And the Shadow . . . the Shadow is That Which Ends All—man, hope, good. To Which there is no appeal, and

Which holds a vast and enduring hatred for that which has life and full substance."

"So Zahur has this new magic. Is it the gift of Shades or Shadow?" Ross brought them back to the subject which had sparked in him a small warning signal.

"Zahur prospers mightily." Loketh's answer was ambiguous.

"And so the Shadow could not provide such magic?" The Terran pushed.

But before the Hawaikan had a chance to answer, Karara added another question:

"But you believe that it did?"

"I do not know. Only the magic has made Zahur a part of Glicmas, and Glicmas is now perhaps a part of that which spoke from the mountain. It is not well to accept gifts which tie one man to another unless there is from the first a saying of how deep that bond may run."

"I think you are wise in that, Loketh," Karara said.

But the uneasiness had grown in Ross. Alien powers, out of a mountain heart, passed from one lord to another. And on the other hand the Rovers' sudden magic in turn, lending their ships wings. The two facts balanced in an odd way. Back on Terra there had been those sudden and unaccountable jumps in technical knowledge on the part of the enemy, jumps which had set in action the whole Time Travel service of which he had become a part. And these jumps had not been the result of normal research; they had come from the looting of derelict spaceships wrecked on his world in the far past.

Could dribbles of the same stellar knowledge have been here deliberately fed to warring communities? He asked Loketh about the possibility of space-borne explorers. But to the Hawaikan that was a totally foreign conception. The stars, for Loketh, were the doorways and windows of the Shades, and he treated the suggestion of space travel as perhaps natural to those all-powerful specters, but certainly not for beings like himself. There was no hint that Hawaika had been openly visited by a galactic ship. Though that did not bar such landings. The planet was, Ross thought, thinly populated. Whole sections of the interiors of the larger islands were wilderness, and this world must be in the same state of only partial occupation as his own earth had been in the Bronze Age when tribes on the march had fanned out into virgin wilderness, great forests, and steppes unwalked by man before their coming.

Now as he balanced in the canoe and tried to keep his mind off the queasiness in his middle and the insecurity of the one thickness of sea-creature hide stretched over a bone framework which made up the craft between his person and the water, Ross still mulled over what might be true. Had the galactic invaders for their own purposes begun to meddle here, leaking weapons or tools to upset what must be a very delicate balance of power? Why? To bring on a conflict which would occupy the native population to the point of exhaustion or depopulation? So they could win a world for their own purposes without effort or risk on their part? Such cold-blooded fishing in carefully troubled waters fitted very well with the persons of the Baldies as he had known them on Terra.

And he could not set aside that memory of this very coast as he had seen it through the peep, the castle in ruins, tall pylons reaching from the land into the sea. Was this the beginning of that change which would end in the Hawaika of his own time, empty of intelligent life, shattered into a loose network of islands?

"This fog is strange." Karara's words startled Ross to return to the here and now.

The haze he had been only half conscious of when they had put out from the tiny secret bay where Loketh kept his boat, was truly a fog, piling up in soft billows and cutting down visibility with speed.

"The Foanna!" Loketh's answer was sharp, a recognition of danger. "Their magic—they hide their place so! There is trouble, trouble on the move!"

"Do we land then?" Ross did not ascribe the present blotting out of the landscape to any real manipulation of nature on the part of the all-powerful Foanna. Too many times the reputations of "medicine men" had been so enhanced by coincidence. But he did doubt the wisdom of trying to bore ahead blindly in this murk.

"Taua and Tino-rau can guide us," Karara reminded him. "Throw out the rope, Ross. What is above water will not confuse them."

He moved cautiously, striving to adapt his actions to the swing of the boat. The line was ready coiled to hand and he tossed the loose end overboard, to feel the cord jerk taut as one of the dolphins caught it up.

They were being towed now, though both paddlers reinforced the forward tug with their efforts. The curtain gathering above the surface of the water did not hamper the swimmers beneath its surface, and Ross felt relief. He turned his head to speak to Loketh.

"How near are we?"

The mist had thickened to the point that, close as the native was, the lines of his body blurred. His clicking answer seemed distorted, too, almost as if the fog had altered not only his form but his personality.

"Maybe very soon now. We must see the sea gate before we are sure."

"And if we aren't able to see that?" challenged Ross.

"The sea gate is above and below the water. Those who obey the Sea Maid, who are able to speak thought to thought, will find it if we can not."

But they were never to reach that goal. Karara gave warning: "There are ships about."

Ross knew that the dolphins had told her. He demanded in turn: "What kind?"

"Larger, much larger than this."

Then Loketh broke in: "A Rover Raider—three of them!"

Ross frowned. He was the cripple here. The other two, with their ability to communicate with the dolphins, were the sighted, he the blind. And he resented his handicap in a burst of bitterness which must have colored his tone as he ordered, "Head inshore—now!"

Once on land, even in the fog, he felt that they had the advantage in any hide-and-seek which might ensue with this superior enemy force. But afloat he was helpless and vulnerable, a state Ross did not accept easily.

"No," Loketh returned as sharply. "There is no place to land along the cliff."

"We are between two of the ships," Karara reported.

"Your paddles—" Ross schooled his voice to a whisper. "Hold them—don't use them. Let the dolphins take us on. In the fog, if we make no sound, we may get by the ships."

"Right!" Karara agreed, and he heard an assenting grunt from Loketh.

They were moving very slowly. Strong as the dolphins were, they dared not expend all their strength on towing the skiff too fast. Ross thought furiously. Perhaps the sea could be their way of escape if the need arose. He had no idea why raiding ships were moving under the cover of fog into the vicinity of the Foanna citadel. But the Terran's knowledge of tactics led him to guess that this impending visit was not anticipated by the Foanna, nor was it a friendly one. And, as veteran seamen who should normally be wary of fog as thick as this, the Rovers themselves must have a driving reason, or some safeguard which led them here now.

But dared the three spill out of their boat, trust to their swimming ability and that of the dolphins, and invade the Foanna sea gate so? Could they use the coming Rover attack as a cover for their own invasion of the hold? Ross considered that the odds in their favor were beginning to look better.

He whispered his idea and began to prepare their gear. The boat was still headed for the shore the three could not see. But they could hear sounds out of the white cotton wall which told them how completely they were boxed in by the raiders; creaks, whispers, noises Ross could not readily identify, carried across the waves.

Before leaving the cave and beginning this voyage they had introduced Loketh to the use of the gill-pack, made him practice in the depths of the cave pool with one of the extras drawn through the gate among the supplies. Now all three were equipped with the water aid, and they could be gone in the sea before the trap closed.

"The supply net—" Ross warned Karara. A moment or two later there was a small bump against the skiff at his left hand. He cautiously raised the collection of containers and eased the burden into the water, knowing that one of the dolphins would take charge of it.

However, he was not prepared for what happened next. Under him the boat lurched first one way and then the other in sharp jerks as if the dolphins were trying to spill them into the sea. Ross heard Karara call out, her voice thin and frightened.

"Taua! Tino-rau! They have gone mad! They will not listen!"

The boat raced in a zigzag path. Loketh clutched at Ross, striving to steady him, to keep the boat on an even keel.

"The Foanna—!" Just as Loketh cried out, Karara plunged over the prow of the boat, whether by design or chance Ross did not know.

And then the craft whirled about, smashed side against side with a dark bulk looming out of the fog. Above, Ross heard cries, knew that they had crashed against one of the raiders. He fought to retain his balance, but he had been knocked to the bottom of the boat against Loketh and they struggled together, unable to move during a precious second or two.

Out of the air over their heads dropped a mass of waving strands which enveloped both of them. The stuff was adhesive, slimy. Ross let out a choked cry as the lines tightened about his arms and body, pinioning him.

Those tightened, wove a net. Now he was being drawn up out of the plunging skiff, a helpless captive. His flailing legs, still free of the slimy cords, struck against the side of the larger ship. Then he swung in, over the well of the deck, thudded down on that surface with bruising force, unable to understand anything except that he had been taken prisoner by a very effective device.

Loketh dropped beside him. But Karara was not brought in, and Ross held to that small bit of hope. Had she made it to freedom by dropping into the water before the Rovers netted them? He could see men gathering about him, masked and distorted in the fog. Then he was rolled across the deck, boosted over the edge of a hatch and knew an instant of terror as he fell into the depth below.

How long was he unconscious? It could not have been very long, Ross decided, as he opened his eyes on dark, heard the small sounds of the ship. He lay very still, trying to remember, to gather his wits before he tried to flex his arms. They were held tight to his sides by strands which no longer seemed slimy, but were wrinkling as they dried. There was an odor from them which gagged him. But there was no loosening of those loops in spite of his struggles, which grew more intense as his strength returned. And at last he lay panting, knowing there was no easy way of escape from here.

## IX

## BATTLE TEST

BABBLE OF SPEECH, cries, sounded muffled to Ross, made a mounting clamor on the deck. Had the raiders' ship been boarded? Was it now under attack? He strove to hear and think through the pain in his head, the bewilderment.

"Loketh?" He was certain that the Hawaikan had been dumped into the same hold.

The only answer was a low moan, a mutter from the dark. Ross began to inch his way in that direction. He was no seaman, but during that worm's progress he realized that the ship itself had changed. The vibration which had carried through the planks on which he lay was stilled. Some engine shut off; one portion of his mind put that into familiar terms. Now the vessel rocked with the waves, did not bore through them.

Ross brought up against another body.

"Loketh!"

"Ahhhhh . . . the fire . . . the fire—!" The half-intelligible answer held no meaning for the Terran. "It burns in my head . . . the fire—"

The rocking of the ship rolled Ross away from his fellow prisoner toward the opposite side of the hold. There was a roar of voice, bull strong above the noise on deck, then the sound of feet back and forth there.

"The fire . . . ahhh—" Loketh's voice rose to a scream.

Ross was now wedged between two abutments he could not see and from which his best efforts could not free him. The pitching of the ship was more pronounced. Remembering the two vessels he had seen pounded to bits on the reef, Ross wondered if the same doom loomed for this one. But that disaster had occurred during a storm. And, save for the fog, this had been a calm night, the sea untroubled.

Unless—maybe the shaking his body had received during the past few moments had sharpened his thinking—unless the Foanna had their own means of protection at the sea gate and this was the result. The dolphins . . . What had made Tino-rau and Taua react as they did? And if the Rover ship was out of control, it would be a good time to attempt escape.

"Loketh!" Ross dared to call louder. "Loketh!" He struggled against the drying strands which bound him from shoulder to mid thigh. There was no give in them.

More sounds from the upper deck. Now the ship was answering to direction again. The Terran heard sounds he could not identify, and the ship no longer rocked so violently. Loketh moaned.

As far as Ross could judge, they were heading out to sea.

"Loketh!" He wanted information; he must have it! To be so ignorant of what was going on was unbearable frustration. If they were now prisoners in a ship leaving the island behind . . . The threat of that was enough to set Ross struggling with his bonds until he lay panting with exhaustion.

"Rosss?" Only a Hawaikan could make that name a hiss.

"Here! Loketh?" But of course it was Loketh.

"I am here." The other's voice sounded oddly weak as if it issued from a man drained by a long illness.

"What happened to you?" Ross demanded.

"The fire . . . the fire in my head—eating . . . eating . . ." Loketh's reply came with long pauses between the words.

The Terran was puzzled. What fire? Loketh had certainly reacted to something beyond the unceremonious handling they had received as captives. This whole ship had reacted. And the dolphins . . . But what fire was Loketh talking about?

"I did not feel anything," he stated to himself as well as to the Hawaikan.

"Nothing burning in your head? So you could not think—"

"No."

"It must have been the Foanna magic. Fire eating so that a man is nothing, only that which fire feeds upon!"

Karara! Ross's thoughts flashed back to those few seconds when the dolphins had seemed to go crazy. Karara had then called out something about the Foanna. So the dolphins must have felt this, and Karara, and Loketh. Whatever *it* was. But why not Ross Murdock?

Karara possessed an extra, undefinable sense which gave her contact with the dolphins. Loketh had a mind which those could read in turn. But such communication was closed to Ross.

At first the realization carried with it a feeling of shame and loss. That he did not have what these others possessed, a subtle power beyond the body, a part of mind, was humbling. Just as he had felt shut out and crippled when he had been forced to use the analyzer instead of the sense the others had, so did he suffer now.

Then Ross laughed shortly. All right, sometimes insensitivity could be a defense as it had at the sea gate. Suppose his lack could also be a weapon? He had not been knocked out as the others appeared to be. But for the bad luck of having been captured before the raiders had succumbed, Ross could, perhaps, have been master of this ship by now. He did not laugh now; he smiled sardonically at his own grandiose reaction. No use thinking about what might have been, just file this fact for future reference.

A creaking overhead heralded the opening of the hatch. Light lanced down into the cubby, and a figure swung over and down a side ladder, coming to stand over Ross, feet apart for balancing, accommodating to the swing of the vessel with the ease of long practice.

Thus Ross came face to face with his first representative of the third party in the Hawaikan tangle of power —a Rover.

The seaman was tall, with a heavier development of shoulder and upper arms than the landsmen. Like the guards he wore supple armor, but this had been colored or overlaid with a pearly hue in which other tints wove opaline lines. His head was bare except for a broad, scaled band running from the nape of his neck to the mid-point of his forehead, a band supporting a sharply serrated crest not unlike the erect fin of some Terran fish.

Now as he stood, fists planted on hips, the Rover presented a formidable figure, and Ross recognized in him the air of command. This must be one of the ship's officers.

Dark eyes surveyed Ross with interest. The light from the deck focused directly across the raider's shoulder to catch the Terran in its full glare, and Ross fought the need for squinting. But he tried to give back stare for stare, confidence for self-confidence.

On Terra in the past more than one adventurer's life had been saved simply because he had the will and nerve enough to face his captors without any display of anxiety. Such bravado might not hold here and now, but it was the only weapon Ross had to hand and he used it.

"You—" the Rover broke the silence first, "you are not of the Foanna—" He paused as if waiting an answer—denial or protest. Ross provided neither.

"No, not of the Foanna, nor of the scum of the coast either." Again a pause.

"So, what manner of fish has come to the net of Torgul?" He called an order aloft. "A rope here! We'll have this fish and its fellow out—"

Loketh and Ross were jerked up to the outer deck,

dumped into the midst of a crowd of seamen. The Hawaikan was left to lie but, at a gesture from the officer, Ross was set on his feet. He could see the nature of his bonds now, a network of dull gray strands, shriveled and stinking, but not giving in the least when he made another try at moving his arms.

"Ho—" The officer grinned. "This fish does not like the net! You have teeth, fish. Use them, slash yourself free."

A murmur of applause from the crew answered that mild taunt. Ross thought it time for a countermove.

"I see you do not come too close to those teeth." He used the most defiant words his limited Hawaikan vocabulary offered.

There was a moment of silence, and then the officer clapped his hands together with a sharp explosion of sound.

"You would use your teeth, fish?" he asked and his tone could be a warning.

This was going it blind with a vengeance, but Ross took the next leap in the dark. He had the feeling, which often came to him in tight quarters, that he was being supplied from some hard core of endurance and determination far within him with the right words, the fortunate guess.

"On which one of you?" He drew his lips tight, displaying those same teeth, wondering for one startled moment if he should take the Rover's query literally.

"Vistur! Vistur!" More than one voice called.

One of the crew took a step or two forward. Like Torgul, he was tall and heavy, his over-long arms well muscled. There were scars on his forearms, the seam of one up his jaw. He looked what he was, a very tough fighting man, one who was judged so by peers as seasoned and dangerous.

"Do you choose to prove your words on Vistur, fish?" Again the officer had a formal note in his question, as if this was all part of some ceremony.

"If he meets with me as he stands—no other weapons." Ross flashed back.

Now he had another reaction from them. There were some jeers, a sprinkling of threats as to Vistur's intentions. But Ross caught also the fact that two or three of them had gone silent and were eyeing him in a new and more searching fashion and that Torgul was one of those.

Vistur laughed. "Well said, fish. So shall it be."

Torgul's hand came out, palm up, facing Ross. In its hollow was a small object the Terran could not see clearly. A new weapon? Only the officer made no move to touch it to Ross, the hand merely moved in a series of waves in mid-air. Then the Rover spoke.

"He carries no unlawful magic."

Vistur nodded. "He's no Foanna. And what need have I to fear the spells of any coast crawler? I am Vistur!"

Again the yells of his supporters arose in hearty answer. The statement held more complete and quiet confidence than any wordy boast.

"And I am Ross Murdock!" The Terran matched the Rover tone for tone. "But does a fish swim with its fins bound to its sides? Or does Vistur fear a free fish too greatly to face one?"

His taunt brought the result Ross wanted. The ties were cut from behind, to flutter down as withered, useless strings. Ross flexed his arms. Tight as those thongs had been they had not constricted circulation, and he was ready to meet Vistur. The Terran did not doubt that the Rover champion was a formidable fighter, but he had not had the advantage of going through one of the Agent training courses. Every trick of unarmed fighting known on his own world had been pounded into Ross long ago. His hands and feet could be as deadly weapons as any crook-bladed sword—or gun—provided he could get close enough to use them properly.

Vistur stripped off his weapon belt, put to one side his

helmet, showing that under it his hair was plaited into a braid coiled about the crown of his head to provide what must be an extra padding for that strangely narrowed helm. Then he peeled off his armor, peeled it literally indeed, catching the lower edge of the scaled covering with his hands and pulling it up and over his head and shoulders as one might skin off a knitted garment. Now he stood facing Ross, wearing little more than the Terran's swimming trunks.

Ross had dropped his belt and gill-pack. He moved into the circle the crew had made. From above came a strong light, centering from a point on the mainmast and giving him good sight of his opponent.

Vistur was being urged to make a quick end of the reckless challenger, his supporters shouting directions and encouragement. But if the Rover had confidence, he also possessed the more intelligent and valuable trait of caution in the face of the unknown. He outweighed, apparently outmatched Ross, but he did not rush in rashly as his backers wished him to.

They circled, Ross studying every move of the Rover's muscles, every slight fraction of change in the other's balance. There would be something to telegraph an attack from the other. For he intended to fight purely in defense.

The charge came at last as the crew grew impatient and yelled their impatience to see the prisoner taught a lesson. But Ross did not believe it was that which sent Vistur at him. The Hawaikan simply thought he knew the best way to take the Terran.

Ross ducked so that a hammer blow merely grazed him. But the Terran's stiffened hand swept sidewise in a judo chop. Vistur gave a whooping cry and went to his knees and Ross swung again, sending the Rover flat to the deck. It had been quick but not so vicious as it might have been. The Terran had no desire to kill or even disable Vistur for more than a few minutes. His victim would carry a couple of aching bruises and perhaps a hearty respect for a new mode of fighting from this encounter. He could have as easily been dead had either of those blows landed other than where Ross chose to plant them.

"Ahhhh—"

The Terran swung around, setting his back to the foot of the mast. Had he guessed wrong? With their chosen champion down, would the crew now rush him? He had gambled on the element of fair play which existed in a primitive Terran warrior society after a man-to-man challenge. But he could be wrong. Ross waited, tense. Just let one of them pull a weapon, and it could be his end.

Two of them were aiding Vistur to his feet. The Rover's breath whistled in and out of him with that same whooping, and both of his hands rose unsteadily to his chest. The majority of his fellows stared from him to the slighter Terran as if unable to believe the evidence of their eyes.

Torgul gathered up from the deck the belt and gill-pack Ross had shed in preparation for the fight. He turned the belt around over his forearm until the empty knife sheath was uppermost. One of the crew came forward and slammed back into its proper place the long diver's knife which had been there when Ross was captured. Then the Rover offered belt and gill-pack to Ross. The Terran relaxed. His gamble had paid off; by the present signs he had won his freedom.

"And my swordsman?" As he buckled on the belt Ross nodded at Loketh still lying bound where they had pushed him at the beginning of the fight.

"He is sworn to you?" Torgul asked.

"He is."

"Loose the coast rat then," the Rover ordered. "Now —tell me, stranger, what manner of man are you? Do you come from the Foanna, after all? You have a magic which is not our magic, since the Stone of Phutka did not reveal it on you. Are you from the Shades?"

His fingers moved in the same sign Loketh had once made before Karara. Ross gave his chosen explanation.

"I am from the sea, Captain. As for the Foanna, they are no friend to me, since they hold captive in their keep one who is my brother-kin."

Torgul stared him up and down. "You say you are from the sea. I have been a Rover since I was able to stumble on my two feet across a deck, after the manner and custom of my people, yet I have never seen your like before. Perhaps your coming means ill to me and mine, but by the Law of Battle, you have won your freedom on this ship. I swear to you, however, stranger, that if ill comes from you, then the Law will not hold, and you shall match your magic against the Strength of Phutka. That you shall discover is another thing altogether."

"I will swear any oath you desire of me, Captain, that I have no ill toward you and yours. There is only one wish I hold: to bring him whom I seek out from the Foanna hold before they make him witches' meat."

"That will be a task worthy of any magic you may be able to summon, stranger. We have tasted this night of the power of the sea gate. Though we went in under the Will of Phutka, we were as weeds whirled about on the waves. Who enters that gate must have more force than any we now know."

"And you, too, then have a score to settle with the Foanna?"

"We have a score against the Foanna, or against their magic," Torgul admitted. "Three ships—one island fairing—are gone as if they never were! And those who went with them are of our fleet-clan. There is the work of the Shadow stretching dark and heavy across the sea, new come into these waters. But there remains nothing we can do this night. We have been lucky to win to sea again. Now, stranger, what shall we do with you? Or will you take to the sea again since you name it as home?"

"Not here," Ross countered swiftly. He must gain some idea of where they might be in relation to the island, how far from its shore. Karara and the dolphins—what had happened to them?

"You took no other prisoners?" Ross had to ask.

"There were more of you?" Torgul countered.

"Yes." No need to say how many, Ross decided.

"We saw no others. You . . . all of you—" the Captain rounded on the still-clustered crew, "get about your work! We must raise Kyn Add by morning and report to the council."

He walked away and Ross, determined to learn all he could, followed him into the stern cabin. Here again the Terran was faced with barbaric splendor in carvings, hangings, a wealth of plate and furnishing not too different from the display he had seen in the Wreckers' castle. As Ross hesitated just within the doorway Torgul glanced back at him.

"You have your life and that of your man, stranger. Do not ask more of me, unless you have that within your hands to enforce the asking."

"I want nothing, save to be returned to where you took me, Captain."

Torgul smiled grimly. "You are from the sea, you yourself said that. The sea is wide, but it is all one. Through it you must have your own paths. Take any you choose. But I do not risk my ship again into what lies in wait before the gates of the Foanna."

"Where do you go then, Captain?"

"To Kyn Add. You have your own choice, stranger—the sea or our fairing."

There would be no way of changing the Rover's decision, Ross thought. And even with the gill-pack he could not swim back to where he had been taken.

There were no guideposts in the sea. But a longer acquaintance with Torgul might be helpful.

"Kyn Add then, Captain." He made the next move to prove equality and establish himself with this Rover, seating himself at the table as one who had the right to share the Captain's quarters.

## X

## DEATH AT KYN ADD

THE HOUR WAS close to dawn again and a need for sleep weighted Ross's eyelids, was a craving as strong as hunger. Still restlessness had brought him on deck, sent him to pacing, alert to this vessel and its crew.

He had seen the ships of the Terran Bronze Age traders—small craft compared to those of his own time, depending upon oarsmen when the wind failed their sails, creeping along coasts rather than venturing too far into dangerous seas, sometimes even tying up at the shore each night. There had been other ships, leaner, hardier. Those had plunged into the unknown, touching lands beyond the sea mists, sailed and oared by men plagued by the need to learn what lay beyond the horizon.

And here was such a ship, taut, well kept, larger than the Viking longboats Ross had watched on the tapes of the Project's collection, yet most like those far-faring Terran craft. The prow curved up in a mighty bowsprit where was the carved likeness of the sea dragon Ross had fought in the Hawaika of his own time. The eyes of that monster flashed with a regular blink of light which the Terran did not understand. Was it a signal or merely a device to threaten a possible enemy?

There were sails, now furled as this ship bored on, answering to the steady throb of what could only be an engine. And his puzzlement held. A Viking longboat powered by motors? The mixture was incongruous.

The crew were uniform as to face. All of them wore

the flexible pearly armor, the skull-strip helmets. Though there were individual differences in ornaments and the choice of weapons. The majority of the men did carry curve-pointed swords, though those were broader and heavier than those the Terran had seen ashore. But several had axes with sickle-shaped heads, whose points curved so far back that they nearly met to form a circle.

Spaced at regular intervals on deck were boxlike objects fronting what resembled gun ports. And smaller ones of the same type were on the raised deck at the stern and mounted in the prow, their muzzles, if the square fronts might be deemed muzzles, flanking the blinking dragon head. Catapults of some type? Ross wondered.

"Ross—" His name was given the hiss Loketh used, but it was not the Wrecker youth who joined him now at the stern of the ship. "Ho . . . that was strong magic, that fighting knowledge of yours!"

Vistur rubbed his chest reminiscently. "You have big magic, sea man. But then you serve the Maid, do you not? Your swordsman has told us that even the great fish understand and obey her."

"Some fish," qualified Ross.

"Such fish as that, perhaps?" Vistur pointed to the curling wake of foam.

Startled, Ross stared in that direction. Torgul's command was the centermost in a trio of ships, and those cruised in a line, leaving three trails of troubled wave behind them. Coming up now to port in the comparative calm between two wakes was a dark object. In the limited light Ross could be sure of nothing save that it trailed the ships, appeared to rest on or only lightly in the water, and that its speed was less than that of the vessels it doggedly pursued.

"A fish—that?" Ross asked.

"Watch!" Vistur ordered.

But the Hawaikan's sight must have been keener than

the Terran's. Had there been a quick movement back there? Ross could not be sure.

"What happened?" He turned to Vistur for enlightenment.

"As a salkar it leaps now and then above the surface. But that is no salkar. Unless, Ross, you who say you are from the sea have servants unlike any finned one we have drawn in by net or line before this day."

The dolphins! Could Tino-rau or Taua or both be in steady pursuit of the ships? But Karara . . . Ross leaned against the rail, stared until his eyes began to water from the strain of trying to make out the nature of the black blot. No use, the distance was too great. He brought his fist down against the wood, trying to control his impatience. More than half of him wanted to burst into Torgul's quarters, demand that the Captain bring the ship about to pick up or contact the trailer or trailers.

"Yours?" again Vistur asked.

Ross had tight rein on himself now. "I do not know. It could well be."

It could well be also that the smart thing would be to encourage the Rovers to believe that he had a force of sea dwellers much larger than the four Time castaways. The leader of an army—or a navy—had more prestige in any truce discussion than a member of a lost scouting party. But the thought that the dolphins could be trailing held both promise and worry—promise of allies, and worry over what had happened to Karara. Had she, too, disappeared after Ashe into the hold of the Foanna?

The day did not continue to lighten. Though there was no cottony mist as had enclosed them the night before, there was an odd muting of sea and sky, limiting vision. Shortly Ross was unable to sight the follower or followers. Even Vistur admitted he had lost visual contact. Had the blot been hopelessly outdistanced, or was it still dogging the wakes of the Rover ships?

Ross shared the morning meal with Captain Torgul, a

round of leathery substance with a salty, meaty flavor, and a thick mixture of what might be native fruit reduced to a tart paste. Once before he had tasted alien food when in the derelict spaceship it had meant eat or starve. And this was a like circumstance, since their emergency ration supplies had been lost in the net. But though he was apprehensive, no ill effects followed. Torgul had been uncommunicative earlier; now he was looser of tongue, volunteering that they were almost to their port—the fairing of Kyn Add.

The Terran had no idea how far he might question the Hawaikan, yet the fuller his information the better. He discovered that Torgul appeared willing to accept Ross's statement that he was from a distant part of the sea and that local customs differed from those he knew.

Living on and by the sea the Rovers were quick-witted, adaptive, with a highly flexible if loose-knit organization of fleet-clans. Each of these had control over certain islands which served them as "fairings," ports for refitting and anchorage between voyages, usually ruggedly wooded where the sea people could find the raw material for their ships. Colonies of clans took to the sea, not in the slim, swift cruisers like the ship Ross was now on, but in larger, deeper vessels providing living quarters and warehouses afloat. They lived by trade and raiding, spending only a portion of the year ashore to grow fast-sprouting crops on their fairing islands and indulge in some manufacture of articles the inhabitants of the larger and more heavily populated islands were not able to duplicate.

Their main article of commerce was, however, a sea-dwelling creature whose supple and well-tanned hide formed their defensive armor and served manifold other uses. This could only be hunted by men trained and fearless enough to brave more than one danger Torgul did not explain in detail. And a cargo of such skins brought enough in trade to keep a normal-sized fleet-clan for a year.

There was warfare among them. Rival clans tried to jump each other's hunting territories, raid fairings. But until the immediate past, Ross gathered, such encounters were relatively bloodless affairs, depending more upon craft and skillful planning to reduce the enemy to a position of disadvantage in which he was forced to acknowledge defeat, rather than ruthless battle of no quarter.

The shore-side Wrecker lords were always considered fair game, and there was no finesse in Rover raids upon them. Those were conducted with a cold-blooded determination to strike hard at a long-time foe. However, within the past year there had been several raids on fairings with the same blood-bath result of a foray on a Wrecker port. And, since all the fleet-clans denied the sneak-and-strike, kill-and-destroy tactics which had finished those Rover holdings, the seafarers were divided in their opinion as to whether the murderous raids were the work of Wreckers suddenly acting out of character and taking to the sea to bring war back to their enemies, or whether there was a rogue fleet moving against their own kind for some purpose no Rover could yet guess.

"And you believe?" Ross asked as Torgul finished his résumé of the new dangers besetting his people.

Torgul's hand, its long, slender fingers spidery to Terran eyes, rubbed back and forth across his chin before he answered:

"It is very hard for one who has fought them long to believe that suddenly those shore rats are entrusting themselves to the waves, venturing out to stir us with their swords. One does not descend into the depths to kick a salkar in the rump; not if one still has his wits safely encased under his skull braid. As for a rogue fleet . . . what would turn brother against brother to the extent of slaying children and women? Raiding for a wife, yes, that is common among our youth. And there have been killings over such matters. But not the killing of a woman—never of a child! We are a people who have never as many women as there are men who wish to bring them into the home cabin. And no clan has as many children as they hope the Shades will send them."

"Then who?"

When Torgul did not answer at once Ross glanced at the Captain, and what the Terran thought he saw showing for an instant in the other's eyes was a revelation of danger. So much so that he blurted out:

"You think that I—we—"

"You have named yourself of the sea, stranger, and you have magic which is not ours. Tell me this in truth: Could you not have killed Vistur easily with those two blows if you had wished it?"

Ross took the bold course. "Yes, but I did not. My people kill no more wantonly than yours."

"The coast rats I know, and the Foanna, as well as any man may know their kind and ways, and my people —But you I do not know, sea stranger. And I say to you as I have said before, make me regret that I suffered you to claim battle rights and I shall speedily correct that mistake!"

"Captain!"

That cry had come from the cabin door behind Ross. Torgul was on his feet with the swift movements of a man called many times in the past for an instant response to emergency.

The Terran was close on the Rover's heels as they reached the deck. A cluster of crewmen gathered on the port side near the narrow bow. That odd misty quality this day held provided a murk hard to pierce, but the men were gesturing at a low-riding object rolling with the waves.

That was near enough for even Ross to be able to distinguish a small boat akin to the one in which he, Karara, and Loketh had dared the sea gate of the Foanna.

Torgul took up a great curved shell hanging by a thong on the mainmast. Setting its narrow end to his lips, he blew. A weird booming note, like the coughing of a sea monster, carried over the waves. But there was no answer from the drifting boat, no sign it carried any passengers.

"Hou, hou, hou—" Torgul's signal was re-echoed by shell calls from the other two cruisers.

"Heave to!" the Captain ordered. "Wakti, Zimmon, Yoana—out and bring that in!"

Three of the crew leaped to the railing, poised there for a moment, and then dived almost as one into the water. A rope end was thrown, caught by one of them. And then they swam with powerful strokes toward the drifting boat. Once the rope was made fast the small craft was drawn toward Torgul's command, the crewmen swimming beside it. Ross longed to know the reason for the tense expectancy of the men around him. It was apparent the skiff had some ominous meaning for them.

Ross caught a glimpse of a body huddled within the craft. Under Torgul's orders a sling was dropped, to rise, weighted with a passenger. The Terran was shouldered back from the rail as the limp body was hurried into the Captain's cabin. Several crewmen slid down to make an examination of the boat itself.

Their heads came up, their eyes searched along the rail and centered on Ross. The hostility was so open the Terran braced himself to meet those cold stares as he would a rush from a challenger.

A slight sound behind sent Ross leaping to the right, wanting to get his back against solid protection. Loketh came up, his limp making him awkward so that he clutched at the rail for support. In his other hand was one of the hooked swords bared and ready.

"Get the murderers!" Someone in the back line of the massing crew yipped that.

Ross drew his diver's knife. Shaken at this sudden change in the crew's attitude, he was warily on the defensive. Loketh was beside him now and the Hawaikan nodded to the sea.

"Better go there," he cried. "Over before they try to gut you!"

"Kill!" The word shrilled into a roar from the Rovers. They started up the deck towards Ross and Loketh. Then someone leaped between, and Vistur fronted his own comrades.

"Stand away—" One of the others ran forward, thrusting at the tall Rover with a stiffened out-held arm to fend him out of their path.

Vistur rolled a shoulder, sending the fellow shunting away. He went down while two more, unable to halt, thudded on him. Vistur stamped on an outstretched hand and sent a sword spinning.

"What goes here!" Torgul's demand was loud enough to be heard. It stopped a few of the crew and two more went down as the Captain struck out with his fists. Then he was facing Ross, and the chill in his eyes was the threat the others had voiced.

"I told you, sea stranger, that if I found you were a danger to me or mine, you would meet the Justice of Phutka!"

"You did," Ross returned. "And in what way am I now a danger, Captain?"

"Kyn Add has been taken by those who are not Wreckers, not Rovers, not those who serve the Foanna—but strangers out of the sea!"

Ross could only stare back, confused. And then the full force of his danger struck home. Who those raiding sea strangers could be, he had no idea, but that he was now condemned out of his own mouth was true and he realized that these men were not going to listen to any argument from him in their present state of mind.

The growl of the crew was that of a hungry animal. Ross saw the wisdom in Loketh's choice. Far better chance the open sea than the mob before them.

But his time for choice had passed. Out of nowhere

whirled a lacy gray-white net, slapping him back against a bulkhead to glue him there. Ross tried to twist loose, got his head around in time to see Loketh scramble to the top of the rail, turn as if to launch himself at the men speeding for the now helpless Terran. But the Hawaikan's crippled leg failed him and he toppled back overside.

"No!" Again Torgul's shout halted the crew. "He shall take the Black Curse with him when he goes to meet the Shadow—and only one can speak that curse. Bring him!"

Helpless, reeling under their blows, dragged along, Ross was thrown into the Captain's cabin, confronted by a figure braced up by coverings and cushions in Torgul's own chair.

A woman, her face a drawn death's head of skin pulled tight upon bone, yet a fiery inner strength holding her mind above the suffering of her body, looked at the Terran with narrowed eyes. She nursed a bandaged arm against her, and now and then her mouth quivered as if she could not altogether control some emotion or physical pain.

"Yours is the cursing, Lady Jazia. Make it heavy to bear for him as his kind has laid the burden of pain and remembering on all of us."

She brought her good hand up to her mouth, wiping its back across her lips as if to temper their quiver. And all the time her eyes held upon Ross.

"Why do you bring me this man?" Her voice was strained, high. "He is not of those who brought the Shadow to Kyn Add."

"What—?" Torgul began and then schooled his voice to a more normal tone. "Those were from the sea?" He was gentle in his questioning. "They came out of the sea, using weapons against which we had no defense?"

She nodded. "Yes, they made very sure that only the dead remained. But I had gone to the Shrine of Phutka, since it was my day of duty, and Phutka's power threw its shade over me. So I did not die, but I saw—yes, I saw!"

"Not those like me?" Ross dared to speak to her directly.

"No, not those like you. There were few . . . only so many—" She spread out her five fingers. "And they were all of one like as if born in one birth. They had no hair on their heads, and their bodies were of this hue—" She plucked at one of the coverings they had heaped around her; it was a lavender-blue mixture.

Ross sucked in his breath, and Torgul was fast to pounce upon the understanding he read in the Terran's face.

"Not your kind—but still you know them!"

"I know them," Ross agreed. "They are the enemy!"

The Baldies from the ancient spaceships, that wholly alien race with whom he had once fought a desperate encounter on the edge of an unnamed sea in the far past of his own world. The galactic voyagers were here—and in active, if secret, conflict with the natives!

## XI

## WEAPON FROM THE DEPTHS

JAZIA TOLD her story with an attention to time and detail which amazed Ross and won his admiration for her breed. She had witnessed the death and destruction of all which was her life, and yet she had the wit to note and record mentally for possible future use all that she had been able to see of the raiders.

They had come out of the sea at dawn, walking with supreme confidence and lack of any fear. Axes flung when they did not reply to the sentries' challenges had never touched them, and a bombardment of heavier missiles had been turned aside. They proved invulnerable to any weapon the Rovers had. Men who made suicidal rushes to use sword or battle ax hand-to-hand had fallen, before they were in striking distance, under spraying tongues of fire from tubes the aliens carried.

Rovers were not fearful or easily cowed, but in the end they had fled from the five invaders, gone to ground in their halls, tried to reach their beached ships, only to die as they ran and hid. The slaughter had been remorseless and entire, leaving Jazia in the hill shrine as the only survivor. She had hidden for the rest of the day, seen the killing of a few fugitives, and that night had stolen to the shore, launched one of the ship's boats which was in a cove well away from the main harbor of the fairing, heading out to sea in hope of meeting the homing cruisers with her warning.

"They stayed there on the island?" Ross asked. That point of her story puzzled him. If the object of that murderous raid had been only to stir up trouble among the Hawaikan Rovers, perhaps turning one clan against the other, as he had deduced when he had listened to Torgul's report of similar happenings, then the star men should have withdrawn as soon as their mission was complete, leaving the dead to call for vengeance in the wrong direction. There would be no reason to court discovery of their true identity by lingering.

"When the boat was asea there were still lights at the fairing hall, and they were not our lights, nor did the dead carry them," she said slowly. "What have those to fear? They can not be killed!"

"If they are still there, that we can put to the test," Torgul replied grimly, and a murmur from his officers bore out his determination.

"And lose all the rest of you?" Ross retorted coldly. "I have met these before; they can will a man to obey them. Look you—" He slammed his left hand flat on the table. The ridges of scar tissue were plain against his tanned skin. He knew no better way of driving home the dangers of dealing with the star men than providing this graphic example. "I held my own hand in fire so that the hurt of it would work against their pull upon my thoughts, against their willing that I come and be easy meat for their butchering."

Jazia's fingers flickered out, smoothed across his old scars lightly as she gazed into his eyes.

"This, too, is true," she said slowly. "For it was also pain of body which kept me from their last snare. They stood by the hall and I saw Prahad, Okun, Mosaji, come out to them to be killed as if they were in a hold net and were drawn. And there was that which called me also so that I would go to them though I called upon the Power of Phutka to save. And the answer to that plea came in a strange way, for I fell as I went from the shrine and cut my arm on the rocks. The paint of that hurt was as a knife severing the net. Then I crawled for the wood and that calling did not come again—"

"If you know so much about them, tell us what

weapons we may use to pull them down!" That demand came from Vistur.

Ross shook his head. "I do not know."

"Yet," Jazia mused, "all things which live must also die sooner or later. And it is in my mind that these have also a fate they dread and fear. Perhaps we may find and use it."

"They came from the sea—by a ship, then?" Ross asked. She shook her head.

"No, there was no ship; they came walking through the breaking waves as if they had followed some road across the sea bottom."

"A sub!"

"What is that?" Torgul demanded.

"A type of ship which goes under the waves, not through them, carrying air within its hull for the breathing of the crew."

Torgul's eyes narrowed. One of the other captains who had been summoned from the two companion cruisers gave a snort of disbelief.

"There are no such ships—" he began, to be silenced by a gesture from Torgul.

"We know of no such ships," the other countered. "But then we know of no such devices as Jazia saw in operation either. How does one war upon these under-the-sea ships, Ross?"

The Terran hesitated. To describe to men who knew nothing of explosives the classic way of dealing with a sub via depth charges was close to impossible. But he did his best.

"Among my people one imprisons in a container a great power. Then the container is dropped near the sub and—"

"And how," broke in the skeptical captain, "do you know where such a ship lies? Can you see it through the water?"

"In a way—not see, but hear. There is a machine which makes for the captain of the above-seas ship a picture of where the sub lies or moves so that he may follow its course. Then when he is near enough he drops the container and the power breaks free—to also break apart the sub."

"Yet the making of such containers and the imprisoning of the power within them," Torgul said, "this is the result of a knowledge with is greater than any save the Foanna may possess. You do not have it?" His conclusion was half statement, half question.

"No, it took many years and the combined knowledge of many men among my people to make such containers, such a listening device. I do not have it."

"Why then think of what we do not have?" Torgul's return was decisive. "What *do* we have?"

Ross's head came up. He was listening, not to anything in that cabin, but to a sound which had come through the port just behind his head. There—it had come again! He was on his feet.

"What—?" Vistur's hand hovered over the ax at his belt. Ross saw their gaze centered on him.

"We may have reinforcements now!" The Terran was already on his way to the deck.

He hurried to the rail and whistled, the thin, shrill summons he had practiced for weeks before he had ever begun this fantastic adventure.

A sleek dark body broke water and the dolphin grin was exposed as Tino-rau answered his call. Though Ross's communication powers with the two finned scouts was very far from Karara's, he caught the message in part and swung around to face the Rovers who had crowded after him.

"We have a way now of learning more about your enemies."

"A boat—it comes without sail or oars!" One of the crew pointed.

Ross waved vigorously, but no hand replied from the skiff. Though it came steadily onward, the three cruisers its apparent goal.

"Karara!" Ross called.

Then side by side with Tino-rau were two wet heads, two masked faces showing as the swimmers trod water —Karara and Loketh.

"Drop ropes!" Ross gave that order as if he rather than Torgul commanded. And the Captain himself was one of those who moved to obey.

Loketh came out of the sea first and as he scrambled over the rail he had his sword ready, looking from Ross to Torgul. The Terran held up empty hands and smiled.

"No trouble now."

Loketh snapped up his mask. "So the Sea Maid said the finned ones reported. Yet before, these thirsted for your blood on their blades. What magic have you worked?"

"None. Just the truth has been discovered." Ross reached for Karara's hand as she came nimbly up the rope, swung her across the rail to the deck where she stood unmasked, brushing back her hair and looking around with a lively curiosity.

"Karara, this is Captain Torgul," Ross introduced the Rover commander who was staring round-eyed at the girl. "Karara is she who swims with the finned ones, and they obey her." Ross gestured to Tino-rau. "It is Taua who brings the skiff?" he asked the Polynesian.

She nodded. "We followed from the gate. Then Loketh came and said that . . . that . . ." She paused and then added, "But you do not seem to be in danger. What has happened?"

"Much. Listen—this is important. There is trouble at an island ahead. The Baldies were there; they murdered the kin of these men. The odds are they reached there by some form of sub. Send one of the dolphins to see what is happening and if they are still there . . ."

Karara asked no more questions, but whistled to the dolphin. With a flip of tail Tino-rau took off.

Since they could make no concrete plan of action, the cruiser captain agreed to wait for Tino-rau's report and to cruise well out of sight of the fairing harbor until it came.

"This belief in magic," Ross remarked to Karara, "has one advantage. The natives seem able to take in their stride the fact the dolphins will scout for us."

"They have lived their lives on the sea; for it they must have a vast respect. Perhaps they know, as did my people, that the ocean has many secrets, some of which are never revealed except to the forms of life which claim their homes there. But, even if you discover this Baldy sub, what will the Rovers be able to do about it?"

"I don't know—yet." Ross could not tell why he clung to the idea that they could do anything to strike back at the superior alien force. He only knew that he was not yet willing to relinquish the thought that in some way they could.

"And Ashe?"

Yes, Ashe . . .

"I don't know." It hurt Ross to admit that.

"Back there, what really happened at the gate?" he asked Karara. "All at once the dolphins seemed to go crazy."

"I think for a moment or two they did. You felt nothing?"

"No."

"It was like a fire flashing through the head. Some protective device of the Foanna, I think."

A mental defense to which he was not sensitive. Which meant that he might be able to breach that gate if none of the others could. But he had to be there first. Suppose, just suppose Torgul could be persuaded that this attack on the gutted Kyn Add was useless. Would the Rover commander take them back to the Foanna keep? Or with the dolphins and the skiff could Ross himself return to make the try?

That he could make it on his own, Ross doubted. Excitement and will power had buoyed him up throughout the past Hawaikan day and night. Now fatigue closed in, past his conditioning and the built-in stimulant of the Terran rations, to enclose him in a groggy haze. He had been warned against this reaction, but that was just another item he had pushed out of his conscious mind. The last thing he remembered now was seeing Karara move through a fuzzy cloud.

Voices argued somewhere beyond, the force of that argument carried more by tone than any words Ross could understand. He was pulled sluggishly out of a slumber too deep for any dream to trouble, and lifted heavy eyelids to see Karara once again. There was a prick in his arm—or was that part of the unreality about him?

"—four—five—six" she was counting, and Ross found himself joining in:

"—seven—eight—nine—ten!"

On reaching "ten" he was fully awake and knew that she had applied the emergency procedure they had been drilled in using, giving him a pep shot. When Ross sat up on the narrow bunk there was a light in the cabin and no sign of day outside the porthole. Torgul, Vistur, the two other cruiser captains, all there . . . and Jazia.

Ross swung his feet to the deck. A pep-shot headache was already beginning, but would wear off soon. There was, however, a concentration of tension in the cabin, and something must have driven Karara to use the drug.

"What is it?"

Karara fitted the medical kit into the compact carrying case.

"Tino-rau has returned. There *is* a sub in the bay. It emits energy waves on a shoreward beam."

"Then they are still there." Ross accepted the dolphin's report without question. Neither of the scouts would make a mistake in those matters. Energy waves beamed shoreward—power for some type of unit the Baldies were using? Suppose the Rovers could find a way of cutting off the power.

"The Sea Maid has told us that this ship sits on the bottom of the harbor. If we could board it—" began Torgul.

"Yes!" Vistur brought his fist down against the end of the bunk on which the Terran still sat, jarring the dull, drug-borne pain in Ross's head. "Take it—then turn it against its crew!"

There was an eagerness in all Rover faces. For that was a game the Hawaikan seafarers understood: Take an enemy ship and turn its armament against its companions in a fleet. But that plan would not work out. Ross had a healthy respect for the technical knowledge of the galactic invaders. Of course he, Karara, even Loketh might be able to reach the sub. Whether they could then board her was an entirely different matter.

Now the Polynesian girl shook her head. "The broadcast there—Tino-rau rates it as lethal. There are dead fish floating in the bay. He had warning at the reef entrance. Without a shield, there will be no way of getting in."

"Might as well wish for a depth bomb," Ross began and then stopped.

"You have thought of something?"

"A shield—" Ross repeated her words. It was so wild this thought of his, and one which might have no chance of working. He knew almost nothing about the resources of the invaders. Could that broadcast which protected the sub and perhaps activated the weapons of the invaders ashore be destroyed? A wall of fish—sea life herded in there as a shield . . . wild, yes, even so wild it might work. Ross outlined the idea, speaking more to Karara than to the Rovers.

"I do not know," she said doubtfully. "That would need many fish, too many to herd and drive—"

"Not fish," Torgul cut in, "salkars!"

"Salkars?"

"You have seen the bow carving on this ship. That is a salkar. Such are larger than a hundred fish! Salkars driven in . . . they might even wreck this undersea ship with their weight and anger."

"And you can find these salkars near-by?" Ross began to take fire. That dragon which had hunted him—the bulk of the thing was well above any other sea life he had seen here. And to its ferocity he could give testimony.

"At the spawning reefs. We do not hunt at this season which is the time of the taking of mates. Now, too, they are easily angered so they will even attack a cruiser. To slay them at present is a loss, for their skins are not good. But they would be ripe for battle were they to be disturbed."

"And how would you get them from the spawning reefs to Kyn Add?"

"That is not too difficult; the reef lies here." Torgul drew lines with the point of his sword on the table top. "And here is Kyn Add. Salkars have a great hunger at this time. Show them bait and they will follow; especially will they follow swimming bait."

There were a great many holes in the plan which had only a halfway chance of working. But the Rovers seized upon it with enthusiasm, and so it was set up

Perhaps some two hours later Ross swam toward the land mass of Kyn Add. Gleams of light pricked on the shore well to his left. Those must mark the Rover settlement. And again the Terran wondered why the invaders had remained there. Unless they knew that there had been three cruisers out on a raid and for some reason they were determined to make a complete mop-up.

Karara moved a little to his right, Taua between them, the dolphin's super senses their guide and warning. The swiftest of the cruisers had departed, Loketh on board to communicate with Tino-rau in the water. Since the male dolphin was the best equipped to provide a fox for salkar hounds, he was the bait for this weird fishing expedition.

"No farther!" Ross's sonic pricked a warning against his body. Through that he took a jolt which sent him back, away from the bay entrance.

"On the reef." Karara's tapped code drew on a new course. Moments later they were both out of the water, though the wash of waves over their flippered feet was constant. The rocks among which they crouched were a rough harborage from which they could see the shore as a dark blot. But they were well away from the break in the reef through which, if their outlandish plan succeeded, the salkars would come.

"A one-in-a-million chance!" Ross commented as he put up his mask.

"Was not the whole Time Agent project founded on just such chances?" Karara asked the right question. This was Ross's kind of venture. Yes, one-in-a-million chances had been pulled off by the Time Agents. Why, it had been close to those odds against their ever finding what they had first sought along the back trails of time—the wrecked spaceships.

Just suppose this could be a rehearsal for another attack? If the salkars could be made to crack the guard of the Baldies, could they also be used against the Foanna gate? Maybe . . . But take one fight at a time.

"They come!" Karara's fingers gripped Ross's shoulder. Her hand was hard, bar rigid. He could see nothing, hear nothing. That warning must have come from the dolphins. But so far their plan was working; the monsters of the Hawaikan sea were on their way.

## XII

## BALDIES

"OHHHH!" Karara clutched at Ross, her breath coming in little gasps, giving vent to her fear and horror. They had not known what might come from this plan; certainly neither had foreseen the present chaos in the lagoon.

Perhaps the broadcast energy of the enemy whipped the already vicious-tempered salkars into this insane fury. But now the moonlit water was beaten into foam as the creatures fought there, attacking each other with a ferocity neither Terran had witnessed before.

Lights gleamed along the shore where the alien invaders must have been drawn by the clamor of the fighting marine reptiles. Somewhere in the heights above the beach of the lagoon a picked band of Rovers should now be making their way from the opposite side of Kyn Add under strict orders not to go into attack unless signaled. Whether the independent sea warriors would hold to that command was a question which had worried Ross from the first.

Tino-rau and Taua in the waters to the seaward of the reef, the two Terrans on that barrier itself, and between them and the shore the wild melee of maddened salkars. Ross started. The sonic warning which had been pulsing steadily against his skin cut off sharply. The broadcast in the bay had been silenced! This was the time to move, but no swimmer could last in the lagoon itself.

"Along the reef," Karara said.

That would be the long way round, Ross knew, but

the only one possible. He studied the cluster of lights ashore. Two or three figures moved there. Seemingly the attention of the aliens was well centered upon the battle still in progress in the lagoon.

"Stay here!" he ordered the girl. Adjusting his mask, Ross dropped into the water, cutting away from the reef and then turning to swim parallel with it. Tino-rau matched him as he went, guiding Ross to a second break in the reef, toward the shore some distance from where the conflict of the salkars made a hideous din in the night.

The Terran waded in the shallows, stripping off his flippers and snapping them to his belt, letting his mask swing free on his chest. He angled toward the beach where the aliens had been. At least he was better armed for this than he had been when he had fronted the Rovers with only a diver's knife. From the Time Agent supplies he had taken the single hand weapon he had long ago found in the armory of the derelict spaceship. This could only be used sparingly, since they did not know how it could be recharged, and the secret of its beam still remained secret as far as Terran technicians were concerned.

Ross worked his way to a curtain of underbrush from which he had a free view of the beach and the aliens. Three of them he counted, and they were Baldies, all right—taller and thinner than his own species, their bald heads gray-white, the upper dome of their skulls overshadowing the features on their pointed chinned faces. They all wore the skintight blue-purple-green suits of the space voyagers—suits which Ross knew of old were insulated and protective for their wearers, as well as a medium for keeping in touch with one another. Just as he, wearing one, had once been trailed over miles of wilderness.

To him, all three of the invaders looked enough alike to have been stamped out from one pattern. And their movements suggested that they worked or went into action with drilled precision. They all faced seaward, holding tubes aimed at the salkar-infested lagoon. There was no sound of any explosion, but green spears of light struck at the scaled bodies plunging in the water. And where those beams struck, flesh seared. Methodically the trio raked the basin. But, Ross noted, those beams which had been steady at his first sighting, were now interrupted by flickers. One of the Baldies upended his tube, rapped its butt against a rock as if trying to correct a jamming. When the alien went into action once again his weapon flashed and failed. Within a matter of moments the other two were also finished. The lighted rods pushed into the sand, giving a glow to the scene, darkened as a fire might sink to embers. Power fading?

An ungainly shape floundered out of the churned water, lumbered over the shale of the beach, its supple neck outstretched, its horned nose down for a gore-threatening charge. Ross had not realized that the salkars could operate out of what he thought was their natural element, but this wild-eyed dragon was plainly bent on reaching its tormentors.

For a moment or two the Baldies continued to front the creature, almost, Ross thought, as if they could not believe that their weapons failed them. Then they broke and ran back to the fairing which they had taken with such contemptuous ease. The salkar plowed along in their wake, but its movements grew more labored the farther it advanced, until at last it lay with only its head upraised, darting it back and forth, its fanged jaws well agape, voicing a coughing howl.

Its plaint was answered from the water as a second of its kind wallowed ashore. A terrible wound had torn skin and flesh just behind its neck; yet still it came on, hissing and bubbling a battle challenge. It did not attack its fellow; instead it dragged its bulk past the first comer, on its way after the Baldies.

The salkars continued to come ashore, two more, a third, a fourth, mangled and torn—pulling themselves as far as they could up the beach. To lie, facing inland, their necks weaving, their horned heads bobbing, their cries a frightful din. What had drawn them out of their preoccupation of battle among themselves into this attempt to reach the aliens, Ross could not determine. Unless the intelligence of the beasts was such that they had been able to connect the searing beams which the Baldies had turned on them so tellingly with the men on the beach, and had responded by striving to reach a common enemy.

But no desire could give them the necessary energy to pull far ashore. Almost helplessly beached, they continued to dig into the yielding sand with their flippers in a vain effort to pursue the aliens.

Ross skirted the clamoring barrier of salkars and headed for the fairing. A neck snapped about; a head was lowered in his direction. He smelled the rank stench of reptile combined with burned flesh. The nearest of the brutes must have scented the Terran in turn, as it was now trying vainly to edge around to cut across Ross's path. But it was completely outclassed on land, and the man dodged it easily.

Three Baldies had fled this way. Yet Jazia had reported five had come out of the sea to take Kyn Add. Two were missing. Where? Had they remained in the fairing? Were they now in the sub? And that sub—what had happened to it? The broadcast had been cut off; he had seen the failure of the weapons and the shore lights. Might the sub have suffered from salkar attack? Though Ross could hardly believe that the beasts could wreck it.

The Terran was traveling blindly, keeping well under cover of such brush as he could, knowing only that he must head inland. Under his feet the ground was rising, and he recalled the nature of this territory as Torgul and Jazia had pictured it for him. This had to be part of the ridge wall of the valley in which lay the buildings of the fairing. In these heights was the Shrine of

Phutka where Jazia had hidden out. To the west now lay the Rover village, so he had to work his way left, downhill, in order to reach the hole where the Baldies had gone to ground. Ross made that progress with the stealth of a trained scout.

Hawaika's moon, triple in size to Terra's companion, was up, and the landscape was sharply clear, with shadows well defined. The glow, weird to Terran eyes, added to the effect of being abroad in a nightmare, and the bellowing of the grounded salkars continued a devils' chorus.

When the Rovers had put up the buildings of their fairing, they had cleared a series of small fields radiating outward from those structures. All of these were now covered with crops almost ready to harvest. The grain, if that Terran term could be applied to this Hawaikan product, was housed in long pods which dipped from shoulder-high bushes. And the pods were well equipped with horny projections which tore. A single try at making his way into one of those fields convinced Ross of the folly of such an advance. He sat back to nurse his scratched hands and survey the landscape.

To go down a very tempting lane would be making himself a clear target for anyone in those buildings ahead. He had seen the flamers of the Baldies fail on the beach, but that did not mean the aliens were now weaponless.

His best chance, Ross decided, was to circle north, come back down along the bed of a stream. And he was at the edge of that watercourse when a faint sound brought him to a frozen halt, weapon ready.

"Rosss—"

"Loketh!"

"And Torgul and Vistur."

This was the party from the opposite side of the island, gone expertly to earth. In the moonlight Ross could detect no sign of their presence, yet their voices sounded almost beside him.

"They are in there, in the great hall." That was Torgul. "But no longer are there any lights."

"Now—" An urgent exclamation drew their attention. Light below. But not the glow of the rods Ross had seen on the beach. This was the warm yellow-red of honest fire, bursting up, the flames growing higher as if being fed with frantic haste.

Three figures were moving down there. Ross began to believe that there were only this trio ashore. He could sight no weapons in their hands, which did not necessarily mean they were unarmed. But the stream ran close behind the rear wall of one of the buildings, and Ross thought its bed could provide cover for a man who knew what he was doing. He pointed out as much to Torgul.

"And if their magic works and you are drawn out to be killed?" The Rover captain came directly to the point.

"That is a chance to be taken. But remember . . . the magic of the Foanna at the sea gate did not work against me. Perhaps this won't either. Once, earlier, I won against it."

"Have you then another hand to give to the fire as your defense?" That was Vistur. "But no man has the right to order another's battle challenge."

"Just so," returned Ross sharply. "And this is a thing I have long been trained to do."

He slid down into the stream bed. Approaching from this angle, the structures of the fairing were between him and the fire. So screened he reached a log wall, got to his feet, and edged along it. Then he witnessed a wild scene. The fire raged in great, sky-touching tongues. And already the roof of one of the Rover buildings smoldered. Why the aliens had built up such a conflagration, Ross could not guess. A signal designed to reach some distance?

He did not doubt there was some urgent purpose. For the three were dragging in fuel with almost frenzied haste, bringing out of the Rover buildings bales of cloth to be ripped apart and whirled into the devouring flames, furniture, everything movable which would burn.

There was one satisfaction. The Baldies were so intent upon this destruction that they kept no watch save that now and then one of them would run to the head of the path leading to the lagoon and listen as if he expected a salkar to come pounding up the slope.

"They're . . . they're rattled!" Ross could hardly believe it. The Baldies who had always occupied his mind and memory as practically invincible supermen were acting like badly frightened primitives! And when the enemy was so off balance you pushed—you pushed hard.

Ross thumbed the button on the grip of the strange weapon. He sighted with deliberation and fired. The blue figure at the top of the path wilted, and for a long moment neither of his companions noted his collapse. Then one of them whirled and started for the limp body, his colleague running after him. Ross allowed them to reach his first victim before he fired the second and third time.

All three lay quiet, but still Ross did not venture forth until he had counted off a dozen Terran seconds. Then he slipped forward keeping to cover until he came up to the bodies.

The blue-clad shoulder had a flaccid feel under his hand as if the muscles could not control the flesh about them. Ross rolled the alien over, looked down in the bright light of the fire into the Baldy's wide-open eyes. Amazement—the Terran thought he could read that in the dead stare which answered his intent gaze—and then anger, a cold and deadly anger which chilled into ice.

"Kill!"

Ross slewed around, still down on one knee, to face the charge of a Rover. In the firelight the Hawaikan's eyes were blazing with fanatical hatred. He had his hooked sword ready to deliver a finishing stroke. The Terran blocked with a shoulder to meet the Rover's knees, threw him back. Then Ross landed on top of the fighting crewman, trying to pin the fellow to earth and avoid that recklessly slashing blade.

"Loketh! Vistur!" Ross shouted as he struggled.

More of the Rovers appeared from between the buildings, bearing down on the limp aliens and the two fighting men. Ross recognized the limping of Loketh using a branch to aid him into a running scuttle across the open.

"Loketh—here!"

The Hawaikan covered the last few feet in a dive which carried him into Ross and the Rover. "Hold him," the Terran ordered and had just time enough to throw himself between the Baldies and the rest of the crew. There was a snarling from the Rovers; and Ross, knowing their temper, was afraid he could not save the captives which they considered, fairly, their legitimate prey. He must depend upon the hope that there were one or two cooler heads among them with enough authority to restrain the would-be-avengers. Otherwise he would have to beam them into helplessness.

"Torgul!" he shouted.

There was a break in the line of runners speeding for him. The big man lunging straight across could only be Vistur; the other, yelling orders, was Torgul. It would depend on how much control the Captain had over his men. Ross scrambled to his feet. He had clicked on the beamer to its lowest frequency. It would not kill, but would render its victim temporarily paralyzed; and how long that state would continue Ross had no way of knowing. Tried on Terran laboratory animals, the time had varied from days to weeks.

Vistur used the flat side of his war ax, clapping it against the foremost runners, setting his own bulk to impose a barrier. And now Torgul's orders appeared to be getting through, more and more of the men slacked, leaving a trio of hot-heads, two of whom Vistur sent reeling with his fists.

The Captain came up to Ross. "They are alive then?" He leaned over to inspect the Baldy the Terran had rolled on his back, assessing the alien's frozen stare with thoughtful measurement.

"Yes, but they can not move."

"Well enough." Torgul nodded. "They shall meet the Justice of Phutka after the Law. I think they will wish that they had been left to the boarding axes of angry men."

"They are worth more alive than dead, Captain. Do you not wish to know why they have carried war to your people, how many of them there may yet be to attack—and other things? Also—" Ross nodded at the fire now catching the second building, "why they have built up that blaze? Is it a signal to others of their kind?"

"Very well said. Yes, it would be well for us to learn such things. Nor will Phutka be jealous of the time we take to ask questions and get answers, many answers." He prodded the Baldy with the toe of his sea boot. "How long will they remain so? Your magic has a bite in it."

Ross smiled. "Not my magic, Captain. This weapon was taken from one of their own ships. As to how long they will remain so—that I do not know."

"Very well, we can take precautions." Under Torgul's orders the aliens were draped with capture nets like those Ross and Loketh had worn. The sea-grown plant adhered instantly, wet strands knitting in perfect restrainers as long as it was uncut.

Having seen to that, Torgul ordered the excavation of Kyn Add.

"As you say," he remarked to Ross, "that fire may well be a signal to bring down more of their kind. I think we have had the Favor of Phutka in this matter, but the prudent man stretches no favor of that kind too far. Also," he looked about him—"we have given to Phutka and the Shades our dead; there is nothing for us here now but hate and sorrow. In one day we have been broken from a clan of pride and ships to a handful of standardless men."

"You will join some other clan?" Karara had come with Jazia to stand on the stone ledge chipped to form a base for a column bearing a strange, brooding-eyed head looking seaward. The Rover woman was superintending the freeing of the head from the column.

At the Terran girl's question the Captain gazed down into the dreadful chaos of the valley. They could yet hear the roars of the dying salkars. The reptiles that had made their way to land had not withdrawn but still lay, some dead now, some with weaving heads reaching inland. And the whole of the fairing was ablaze with fire.

"We are now blood-sworn men, Sea Maid. For such there is no clan. There is only the hunting and the kill. With the magic of Phutka perhaps we shall have a short hunt and a good kill."

"There . . . now . . . so . . ." Jazia stepped back. The head which had faced the sea was lowered carefully to a wide strip of crimson-and-gold stuff she had brought from Torgul's ship. With her one usable hand the Rover woman drew the fabric about the carving, muffling it except for the eyes. Those were large ovals deeply carved, and in them Ross saw a glitter. Jewels set there? Yet, he had a queer, shivery feeling that something more than gems occupied those sockets—that he had actually been regarded for an instant of time, assessed and dismissed.

"We go now." Jazia waved and Torgul sent men forward. They lifted the wrapped carving to a board carried between them and started downslope.

Karara cried out and Ross looked around.

The pillar which had supported the head was crumbling away, breaking into a rubble which cascaded across the stone ledge. Ross blinked—this must be an illusion, but he was too tired to be more than dully amazed as he became one of the procession returning to the ships.

## XIII

## THE SEA GATE OF THE FOANNA

Ross RAISED a shell cup to his lips but hardly sipped the fiery brew it contained. This was a gesture of ceremony, but he wanted a steady head and a quick tongue for any coming argument. Torgul, Afrukta, Ongal—the three commanders of the Rover cruisers; Jazia, who represented the mysterious Power of Phutka; Vistur and some other subordinate officers; Karara; himself, with Loketh hovering behind: a council of war. But summoned against whom?

The Terran had come too far afield from his own purpose—to reach Ashe in the Foanna keep. And to further his own plans was a task he doubted his ability to perform. His attack on the Baldies had made him too important to the Rovers for them to allow him willingly to leave them on a quest of his own.

"These star men"—Ross set down the cup, tried to choose the most telling words in his limited Hawaikan vocabulary—"possess weapons and powers you can not dream of, that you have no defense against. Back at Kyn Add we were lucky. The salkars attacked their sub and halted the broadcast powering their flamers. Otherwise we could not have taken them, even though we were many against their few. Now you talk of hunting them in their own territory—on land and in the mountains where they have their base. That would be folly akin to swimming bareheaded to front a salkar."

"So—then we must sit and wait for them to eat us up?" flared Ongal. "I say it is better to die fighting with one's blade wet!"

"Do you not also wish to take at least one of the enemy with you when you fight to that finish?" Ross countered. "These could kill you before you came in blade range."

"You had no trouble with that weapon of yours," Afrutka spoke up.

"I have told you—this weapon was stolen from them. I have only one and I do not know how long it will continue to serve me, or whether they have a defense against it. Those we took were naked to any force, for their broadcast had failed them. But to smash blindly against their main base would be the act of madmen."

"The salkars opened a way for us—" That was Torgul.

"But we can not move a pack of those inland to the mountains," Vistur pointed out reasonably.

Ross studied the Captain. That Torgul was groping for a plan and that it had to be a shrewd one, the Terran guessed. His respect for the Rover commander had been growing steadily since their first meeting. The cruiser-raiders had always been captained by the most daring men of the Rover clans. But Ross was also certain that a successful cruiser commander must possess a level-headed leaven of intelligence and be a strategist of parts.

The Hawaikan force needed a key which would open the Baldy base as the salkars had opened the lagoon. And all they had to aid them was a handful of facts gained from their prisoners.

Oddly enough the picklock to the captives' minds had been produced by the dolphins. Just as Tino-rau and Taua had formed a bridge of communication between the Terran and Loketh, so did they read and translate the thoughts of the galactic invaders. For the Baldies, among their own kind, were telepathic, vocalizing only to give orders to inferiors.

Their capture by these primitive "inferiors" had delivered the first shock, and the mind-probes of the dolphins had sent the "supermen" close to the edge of sanity. To accept an animal form as an equal had been shattering.

But the star men's thoughts and memories had been windowed at last and the result spread before the impromptu council. Rovers and Terrans were briefed on the invaders' master plan for taking over a world. Why they desired to do so even the dolphins had not been able to discover; perhaps they themselves had not been told by their superiors.

It was a plan almost contemptuous in its simplicity, as if the galactic force had no reason to fear effective opposition. Except in one direction—one single direction.

Ross's fingers tightened on the small cup. Had Torgul reached that conclusion yet, the belief that the Foanna could be their key? If so, they might be able to achieve their separate purposes in one action.

"It would seem that they are wary of the Foanna," he suggested, alert to any telltale response from Torgul. But it was Jazia who answered the Terran's half question.

"The Foanna have a powerful magic; they can order wind and wave, man and creature—if so be their will. Well might these killers fear the Foanna!"

"Yet now they move against them," Ross pointed out, still eyeing Torgul.

The Captain's reply was a small, quiet smile.

"Not directly, as you have heard. It is all a part of their plan to set one of us against the other, letting us fight many small wars and so use up our men while they take no risks. They wait the day when we shall be exhausted and then they will reveal themselves to claim all they wish. So today they stir up trouble between the Wreckers and the Foanna, knowing that the Foanna are few. Also they strive in turn to anger us by raids, allowing us to believe that either the Wreckers or Foanna have attacked. Thus—" he held up his left thumb, made a pincers of right thumb and forefinger to close upon it, "they hope to catch the Foanna, between Wreckers and Rovers. Because the Foanna are those they reckon the most dangerous they move against them now, using us and weakening our forces into the bargain. A plan which is clever, but the plan of men who do not like to fight with their own blades."

"They are worse than the coast scum, these cowards!" Ongal spat.

Torgul smiled again. "That is what they believe we will say, kinsman, and so underrate them. By our customs, yes, they are cowards. But what care they for our judgments? Did we think of the salkars when we used them to force the lagoon? No, they were only beasts to be our tools. So now it is the same with us, except that we know what they intend. And we shall not be such obedient tools. If the Foanna are our answer, then—" He paused, gazing into his cup as if he could read some shadowy future there.

"If the Foanna are the answer, then what?" Ross pushed.

"Instead of fighting the Foanna, we must warn, cherish, try to ally ourselves with them. And do all that while we still have time!"

"Just how do we do these things?" demanded Ongal. "The Foanna you would warn, cherish, claim as allies, are already our enemies. Were we not on the way to force their sea gate only days ago? There is no chance of seeking peace now. And have the finned ones not learned from the women-killers that already there is an army of Wreckers camped about the citadel to which these sons of the Shadow plan to lend certain weapons? Do we throw away three cruisers—all we have left—in a hopeless fight? Such is the council of one struck by loss of wits."

"There is a way—my way," Ross seized the opening. "In the Foanna citadel is my sword-lord, to whose service I am vowed. We were on our way to attempt his freeing when your ship picked us out of the waves. He is learned beyond me in the dealing with strange peoples, and if the Foanna are as clever as you say, they will already have discovered that he is not just a slave they claimed from Lord Zahur."

There it was in the open, his own somewhat tattered hope that Ashe had been able to impress his captors with his knowledge and potential. Trained to act as contact man with other races, there was a chance that Gordon had saved himself from whatever fate had been planned for the prisoners the Foanna had claimed. If that happened, Ashe could be their opening wedge in the Foanna stronghold.

"This also I know: That which guards the gate—which turns your minds whirling and sent you back from your raid—does not affect me. I may be able to win inside and find my clansman, and in that doing treat with the Foanna."

The Baldy prisoners had not underestimated the attack on the Foanna citadel. As the Rover cruisers beat in under the cover of night the fires and torches of both besieged and besiegers made a wild glow across the sky. Only on the sea side of the fortress there was no sign of involvement. Whatever guarded the gate must still be in force.

Ross stood with his feet well apart to balance his body against the swing of the deck. His suggestion had been argued over, protested, but at last carried with the support of Torgul and Jazia, and now he was to make his try. The sum of the Rovers' and Loketh's knowledge of the sea gate had been added for his benefit, but he knew that this venture must depend upon himself alone. Karara, the dolphins, the Hawaikans, were all too sensitive to the barrier.

Torgul moved in the faint light. "We are close; our power is ebbing. If we advance, we shall be drifting soon."

"It is time then." Ross crossed to the rope ladder,

but another was there before him. Karara perched on the rail. He regarded her angrily.

"You can't go."

"I know. But we are still safe here. Just because you are free of one defense of the gate, Ross, do not believe that makes it easy."

He was stung by her assumption that he could be so self-assured.

"I know my business."

Ross pushed past her, swinging down the rope ladder, pausing only above water level to snap on flippers, make sure of the set of his weighted belt, and slide his gill-mask over his face. There was a splash beside him as the net containing spare belt, flippers, and mask hit the water and he caught at it. These could provide Ashe's escape from the fortress.

The lights on the shore made a wide arc of radiance across the sea. As Ross headed toward the wave-washed coast he began to hear shouting and other sounds which made him believe that the besiegers were in the midst of an all-out assault. Yet those distant fires and rocket-like blasts into the sky had a wavery blur. And Ross, making his way with the effortless water cleaving of the diver, surfaced now and then to spot film curling up from the surface of the sea between the two standing rock pillars which marked the sea gate.

He was startled by a thunderous crack, rending the air above the small bay. Ross pulled to one of the pillars, steadied himself with one hand against it. Those twists of film rising from the surging surface were thickening. More tendrils grew out from parent stems to creep along above the waves, raising up sprouts and branches in turn. A wall of mist was building between gate and shore.

Again a thunderclap overhead. Involuntarily the Terran ducked. Then he turned his face up to the sky, striving to see any evidence of storm. What hung there sped the growth of the fog on the water. Yet where the fog was gray-white, it was a darkness sprouting from the highest point of the citadel. Ross could not explain how he was able to see one shade of darkness against equal dusk, but he did—or did he only sense it? He shook his head, willing himself to look away from the finger. Only it was a finger no longer; now it was a fist aimed at the stars it was fast blotting out. A fist rising to the heavens before it curled back, descended to press the fortress and its surroundings into rock and earth.

Fog curled about Ross, spilled outward through the sea gates. He loosed his grip on the pillar and dived, swimming on through the gap with the fortress of the Foanna before him.

There was a jetty somewhere ahead; that much he knew from Torgul's description. Those who served the Foanna sometimes took sea roads and they had slim, fast cutters for such coastwise travel. Ross surfaced cautiously, to discover there was no visibility to wave level. Here the mist was thick, a smothering cover so bewildering he was confused as to direction. He ducked below again and flippered on.

Was his confusion born of the fog, or was it also in his head? Did he, after all, have this much reaction to the gate defense? Ross ducked that suspicion as he had ducked the moist blanket on the surface. He had come from the gate, which meant that the jetty must lie—there!

A few moments later Ross had proof that his sense of direction had not altogether failed him, when his shoulder grazed against a solid obstruction in the water and his exploring touch told him that he had found one of the jetty piles. He surfaced again and this time he heard not a thunder roll but the singsong chanting of the Foanna.

It was loud, almost directly above his head, but since the cotton mist held he was not afraid of being sighted. The chanter must be on the jetty. And to Ross's right was a dark bulk which he thought was one of the cutters. Was a sortie by the besieged being planned?

Then, out of the night, came a dazzling beam, well above the level of Ross's head where he clung to the piling. It centered on the cutter, slicing into the substance of the vessel with the ease of steel piercing clay. The chanting stopped on mid-note, broken by cries of surprise and alarm. Ross, pressing against the pile, received a jolt from his belt sonic.

There must be a Baldy sub in the basin inside the gate. Perhaps the flame beam now destroying the cutter was to be turned on the walls of the keep in turn.

Foanna chant again, low and clear. Splashes from the water as those on the jetty cast into the sea objects Ross could not define. The Terran's body jerked, his mask smothered a cry of pain. About his legs and middle, immersed in the waves, there was cold so intense that it seared. Fear goaded him to pull up on one of the under beams of the pier. He reached that refuge and rubbed his icy legs with what vigor he could summon.

Moments later he crept along toward the shore. The energy ray had found another target. Ross paused to watch a second cutter sliced. If the counterstroke of the Foanna would rout the invaders, it had not yet begun to work.

The net holding the extra gear brought along in hopes of Ashe's escape weighed the Terran down, but he would not abandon it as he felt his way from one foot- and hand-hold to the next. The waves below gave off an icy exudation which made him shiver uncontrollably. And he knew that as long as that effect lasted he dared not venture into the sea again.

Light . . . along with the cold, there was a phosphorescence on the water—white patches floating, dipping, riding the waves. Some of them gathered under the pier, clustering about the pilings. And the fog thinned with their coming, as if those irregular blotches absorbed and fed upon the mist. The Terran could see now he had reached the land end of the jetty. He wedged his flippers into his belt, pulled on over his feet the covers of salkar-hide Torgul had provided.

Save for his belt, his trunks, and the gill-pack, Ross's body was bare and the cold caught at him. But, slinging the carry net over his shoulder, he dropped to the damp sand and stood listening.

The clamor of the attack which had carried all the way offshore to the Rover cruisers had died away. And there were no more claps of thunder. Instead, there was now a thick wash of rain.

No more fire rays as he faced seaward. And the fog was lifting, so Ross could distinguish the settling cutters, their bows still moored to the jetty. There was no movement there. Had those on the pier fled?

Dot . . . dash . . . dot . . .

Ross did not drop the net. But he crouched back in the half protection of the piling. For a moment which stretched beyond Terran time measure he froze so, waiting.

Dot . . . dash . . . dot . . .

Not the prickle induced by the enemy installations, it was a real coded call picked up by his sonic, and one he knew.

Don't rush, he told himself sharply—play it safe. By rights only two people in this time and place would know that call. And one would have no reason to use it. But—a trap? This could be a trap. Awe of the Foanna powers had touched him a little in spite of his off-world skepticism. He could be lured now by someone using Ashe's call.

Ross stripped for action after a fashion, bundling the net and its contents into a hollow he scooped behind a pile well above water level. The alien hand weapon he had left with Karara, not trusting it to the sea. But he had his diver's knife and his two hands which, by training, could be, and had been, deadly weapons.

With the sonic against the bare skin of his middle

where it would register strongest, knife in hand, Ross moved into the open. The floating patches did not supply much light, but he was certain the call had come from the jetty.

There was movement there—a flash or two. And the sonic? Ross had to be sure, very sure. The broadcast was certainly stronger when he faced in that direction. Dared he come into the open? Perhaps in the dark he could cut Ashe away from his captors so they could swim for it together.

Ross clicked a code reply. Dot . . . dot . . . dot . . .

The answer was quick, imperative: "Where?"

Surely no one but Ashe could have sent that! Ross did not hesitate.

"Be ready—escape."

"No!" Even more imperative. "Friends here . . ."

Had he guessed rightly? Had Ashe established friendly relations with the Foanna? But Ross kept to the caution which had been his defense and armor so long. There was one question he thought only Ashe could answer, something out of the past they had shared when they had made their first journey into time disguised as Beaker traders of the Bronze Age. Deliberately he tapped that question.

"What did we kill in Britain?"

Tensely he waited. But when the reply came it did not pulse from the sonic under his fingers; instead, a well-remembered voice called out of the night.

"A white wolf." And the words were Terran English.

"Ashe!" Ross leaped forward, climbed toward the figure he could only dimly see.

## XIV

## THE FOANNA

"Ross!" Ashe's hands gripped his shoulders as if never intending to free him again. "Then you did come through—"

Ross understood. Gordon Ashe must have feared that he was the only one swept through the time door by that freak chance.

"And Karara and the dolphins!"

"Here—now?" In this black bowl of the citadel bay Ashe was only a shadow with voice and hands.

"No, out with the Rover cruisers. Ashe, do you know the Baldies are on Hawaika? They've organized this whole thing—the attack here—trouble all over. Right now they have one of their subs out there. That's what cut those cutters to pieces. Five days ago five of them wiped out a whole Rover fairing, just five of them!"

"Gordoon." Unlike the hissing speech of the Hawaikans, this new voice made a singing, lilting call of Ashe's name. "This is your swordsman in truth?" Another shadow drew near them, and Ross saw the flutter of cloak edge.

"This is my friend." There was a tone of correction in Ashe's reply. "Ross, this is the Guardian of the sea gate."

"And you come," the Foanna continued, "with those who gather to feast at the Shadow's table. But your Rovers will find little loot to their liking—"

"No." Ross hesitated. How did one address the Foanna? He had claimed equality with Torgul. But that approach was not the proper one here; instinct told him that. He fell back on the complete truth uttered simply.

"We took three of the Baldy killers. From them we learned they move to wipe out the Foanna first. For you," he addressed himself to the cloaked shape, "they believe to be a threat. We heard that they urged the Wreckers to this attack and so—"

"And so the Rovers come, but not to loot? Then they are something new among their kind." The Foanna's reply was as chill as the sea bay's water.

"Loot does not summon men who want a blood price for their dead kin!" Ross retorted.

"No, and the Rovers are believers in the balance of hurt against hurt," the Foanna conceded. "Do they also believe in the balance of aid against aid? Now that is a thought upon which depends much. Gordoon, it would seem that we may not take to our ships. So let us return to council."

Ashe's hand was on Ross's arm guiding him through the murk. Though the fog which had choked the bay had vanished, thick darkness remained and Ross noted that even the fires and flares were dimmed and fewer. Then they were in a passage where a very faint light clung to the walls.

Robed Foanna, three of them, moved ahead with that particular gliding progress. Then Ashe and Ross, and bringing up the rear, a dozen of the mailed guards. The passageway became a ramp. Ross glanced at Ashe. Like the Foanna, the Terran Agent wore a cloak of gray, but his did not shift color from time to time as did those of the Hawaikan enigmas. And now Gordon shoved back its folds, revealing supple body armor.

Questions gathered in Ross. He wanted to know—needed desperately to know—Ashe's standing with the Foanna. What had happened to raise Gordon from the status of captive in Zahur's hold to familiar companionship with the most dreaded race on this planet?

The ramp's head faced blank wall with a sharp-angled turn to the right of a narrower passage. One of the Foanna made a slight sign to the guards, who turned with drilled precision to march off along the passage. Now the other Foanna held out their wands.

What a moment earlier had been unbroken surface showed an opening. The change had been so instantaneous that Ross had not seen any movement at all.

Beyond that door they passed from one world to another. Ross's senses, already acutely alert to his surroundings, could not supply him with any reason by sight, sound, or smell for his firm conviction that this hold was alien as neither the Wrecker castle nor the Rover ships had been. Surely the Foanna were not the same race, perhaps not even the same species as the other native Hawaikans.

Those robes which he had seen both silver gray and dark blue, now faded, pearled, thinned, until each of the three still gliding before him were opalescent columns without definite form.

Ashe's grasp fell on Ross's arm once more, and his whisper reached the younger man thinly. "They are mistresses of illusion. Be prepared not to believe all that you see."

Mistresses—Ross caught that first. Women, or at least female then. Illusion, yes, already he was convinced that here his eyes could play tricks on him. He could hardly determine what was robe, what was wall, or if more than shades of shades swept before him.

Another blank wall, then an opening, and flowing through it to touch him such a wave of alienness that Ross felt he was buffeted by a storm wind. Yet as he hesitated before it, reluctant in spite of Ashe's hold to go ahead, he also knew that this did not carry with it the cold hostility he had known while facing the Baldies. Alien—yes. Inimical to his kind—no.

"You are right, younger brother."

Spoken those words—or forming in his mind?

Ross was in a place which was sheer wonder. Under his feet dark blue—the blue of a Terran sky at dusk—caught up in it twinkling points of light as if he strode, not equal with stars, but above them! Walls—were there any walls here? Or shifting, swaying blue curtains on which silvery lines ran to form symbols and words which some bemused part of his brain almost understood, but not quite.

Constant motion, no quiet, until he came to a place where those swaying curtains were stilled, where he no longer strode above the sky but on soft surface, a mat of gray living sod where his steps released a spicy fragrance. And there he really saw the Foanna for the first time.

Where had their cloaks gone? Had they tossed them away during that walk or drift across this amazing room, or had the substance which had formed those coverings flowed away by itself? As Ross looked at the three in wonder he knew that he was seeing them as not even their servants and guards ever viewed them. And yet was he seeing them as they really were or as they wished him to see them?

"As we are, younger brother, as we are!" Again an answer which Ross was not sure was thought or speech.

In form they were humanoid, and they were undoubtedly women. The muffling cloaks gone, they wore sleeveless garments of silver which were girded at the waist with belts of blue gems. Only in their hair and their eyes did they betray alien blood. For the hair which flowed and wove about them, cascading down shoulders, rippling about their arms, was silver, too, and it swirled, moved as if it had a separate life of its own. While their eyes . . . Ross looked into those golden eyes and was lost for seconds until panic awoke in him, forcing him after sharp struggle to look away.

Laughter? No, he had not heard laughter. But a sense of amusement tinged with respect came to him.

"You are very right, Gordoon. This one is also of your kind. He is not witches' meat." Ross caught the distaste, the kind of haunting unhappiness which colored those words, remnants of an old hurt.

"These are the Foanna," Ashe's voice broke more of the spell. "The Lady Ynlan, the Lady Yngram, the Lady Ynvalda."

The Foanna—these three only?

She whom Ashe had named Ynlan, whose eyes had entrapped and almost held what was Ross Murdock, made a small gesture with her ivory hand. And in that gesture as well as in the words witches' meat the Terran read the unhappiness which was as much a part of this room as the rest of its mystery.

"The Foanna are now but three. They have been only three for many many years, oh man from another world and time. And soon, if these enemies have their way, they will not be three—but none!"

"But—" Ross was still startled. He knew from Loketh that the Wreckers had deemed the Foanna few in number, an old and dying race. But that there were only three women left was hard to believe.

The response to his unspoken wonder came clear and determined. "We may be but three; however, our power remains. And sometimes power distilled by time becomes the stronger. Now it would seem that time is no longer our servant but perhaps among our enemies. So tell us this tale of yours as to why the Rovers would make one with the Foanna—tell us all, younger brother!"

Ross reported what he had seen, what Tino-rau and Taua had learned from the prisoners taken at Kyn Add. And when he had finished, the three Foanna stood very still, their hands clasped one to the other. Though they were only an arm's distance from him, Ross had the feeling they had withdrawn from his time and world. So complete was their withdrawal that he dared to ask Ashe one of the many questions which had been boiling inside him.

"Who are they?" But Ross knew he really meant: What are they?

Gordon Ashe shook his head. "I don't really know—the last of a very old race which possesses powers and knowledge different from any we have believed in for centuries. We have heard of witches. In the modern day we discount the legends about them. The Foanna bring those legends alive. And I promise you this—if they turn those powers loose"—he paused—"it will be such a war as this world, perhaps any world has never seen."

"That is so." The Foanna had returned from the place to which they had withdrawn. "And this is also the truth or one face of the truth. The Rovers are right in their belief that we have kept some measure of balance between one form of change and another on this world. If we were as many as we once were, then against us these invaders could not move at all. But we are three only and also—do we have the right to evoke disaster which will strike not only the enemy but perhaps recoil upon the innocent? There has been enough death here already. And those who are our servants shall no longer be asked to face battle to keep an empty shell inviolate. We would see with our own eyes these invaders, probe what they would do. There is ever change in life, and if a pattern grows too set, then the race caught in it may wither and die. Maybe our pattern has been too long in its old design. We shall make no decision until we see in whose hands the future may rest."

Against such finality of argument there was no appeal. These could not be influenced by words.

"Gordoon, there is much to be done. Do you take with you this younger brother and see to his needs. When all is in readiness we shall come."

One minute Ross had been standing on the carpet of living moss. Then . . . he was in a more normal room with four walls, a floor, a ceiling, and light which came from rods set in the corners. He gasped.

"Stunned me, too, the first time they put me through it," he heard Ashe say. "Here, get some of this inside you, it'll steady your head."

There was a cup in his hand, a beautifully carved,

rose-red container shaped in the form of a flower. Somehow Ross brought it to his lips with shaking hands, gulped down a good third of its contents. The liquid was a mixture of tart and sweet, cooling his mouth and throat, but warming as it went down, and that glow spread through him.

"What—how did they do that?" he demanded.

Ashe shrugged. "How do they do the hundred and one things I have seen happen here? We've been teleported. How it's done I don't know any more than I did the first time it happened. Simply a part of Foanna 'magic' as far as spectators are concerned." He sat down on a stool, his long legs stretched out before him. "Other worlds, other ways—even if they are confounded queer ones. As far as I know, there's no reason for their power to work, but it does. Now, have you seen the time gate? Is it in working order?"

Ross put down the now empty cup and sat down opposite Ashe. As concisely as he could, he outlined the situation with a quick résumé of all that happened to him, Karara, and the dolphins since they had been sucked through the gate. Ashe asked no questions, but his expression was that of the Agent Ross had known, evaluating and listing all the younger man had to report. When the other was through he said only two words.

"No return."

So much had happened in so short a time that Ross's initial shock at the destruction of the gate had faded, been well overlaid by all the demands made upon his resources, skill, and strength. Even now, the fact Ashe voiced seemed of little consequence balanced against the struggle in progress.

"Ashe—" Ross rubbed his hands up and down his arms, brushing away grains of sand. "Remember those pylons with the empty seacoast behind them? Does that mean the Baldies are going to win?"

"I don't know. No one has ever tried to change the

course of history. Maybe it is impossible even if we dared to try." Ashe was on his feet again, pacing back and forth.

"Try what, Gordoon?"

Ross jerked around, Ashe halted. One of the Foanna stood there, her hair playing about her shoulders as if some breeze felt only by her stirred those long strands.

"Dare to try and change the course of the future," Ashe explained, accepting her materialization with the calm of one who had witnessed it before.

"Ah, yes, your traveling in time. And now you think that perhaps this poor world of ours has a chance as to which overlords it will welcome? I do not know either, Gordoon, whether the future may be altered nor if it be wise to try. But also . . . well, perhaps we should see our enemy before we are set in any path. Now, it is time that we go. Younger brother, how did you plan to leave this place when you accomplished your mission?"

"By the sea gate. I have extra swimming equipment cached under the jetty."

"And the Rover ships await you at sea?"

"Yes."

"Then we shall take your way, since the cutters are sunk."

"There is only one extra gill-pack—and that Baldy sub is out there, too!"

"So? Then we shall try another road, though it will sap our power temporarily." Her head inclined slightly to the left as if she listened. "Good! Our people are now in the passage which will take them to safety. What those outside will find here when they break in will be of little aid to their plans. Secrets of the Foanna remain secrets past others' prying. Though they shall try, oh, how they shall try to solve them! There is knowledge that only certain types of minds can hold and use, and to others it remains for all time unlearnable. Now—"

Her hand reached out, flattened against Ross's forehead.

"Think of your Rover ship, younger brother, see it in your mind! And see well and clearly for me."

Torgul's cruiser was there; he could picture with details he had not thought he knew or remembered. The deck in the dark of the night with only a shaded light at the mast. The deck . . .

Ross gave a choked cry. He did not see this in his mind; he saw it with his eyes! His hand swung out in an involuntary gesture of repudiation and struck painfully against wood. He was on the cruiser!

A startled exclamation from behind him—then a shout. Ashe, Ashe was here and beyond him three cloaked figures, the Foanna. They had their own road indeed and had taken it.

"You . . . Ross—" Vistur fronted them, his face a mixture of bewilderment and awe. "The Foanna—" said in a half whisper, echoed by crewmen gathering around, but not too close.

"Gordon!" Karara elbowed her way between two of the Hawaikans and ran across the deck. She caught the Agent's both hands as if to assure herself that he was alive and there before her. Then she turned to the three Foanna.

There was an odd expression on the Polynesian girl's face, first of measurement with some fear, and then of dawning wonder. From beneath the cloak of the middle Foanna came the rod of office with its sparkling knob. Karara dropped Ashe's hands, took a tentative step forward and then another. The knob was directly before her, breast high. She brought up both hands, cupping them about the knob, but not touching it directly. The sparks it emitted could have been flashing against her flesh, but Karara displayed no awareness of that. Instead, she lifted both hands farther, palm up and cupped, as if she carried some invisible bounty, then flattened them, loosing what she held.

There was a sigh from the crewmen; Karara's gesture had been confident, as if she knew just what she was doing and why. And Ross heard Ashe draw in a deep breath also as the Terran girl turned, allying herself with the Foanna.

"These Great Ones stand in peace," she said. "It is their will that no harm comes to this ship and those who sail in her."

"What do the Great Ones want of us?" Torgul advanced but not too near.

"To speak concerning those who are your prisoners."

"So be it." The Captain bowed. "The Great Ones' will is our will; let it be as they wish."

## XV

## RETURN TO THE BATTLE

Ross LAY listening to the even breathing from across the cabin. He had awakened in that quick transference from sleep to consciousness which was always his when on duty, but he made no attempt to move. Ashe was still sleeping.

Ashe, whom he thought or had thought he knew as well as one man could ever know another, who had taken the place of family for Ross Murdock the loner. Years—two . . . four of them now since he had made half of that partnership.

His head turned, though he could not see that lean body, that quiet, controlled face. Ashe still looked the same, but . . . Ross's sense of loss was hurt and anger mingled. What had they done to Gordon, those three? Bewitched? Tales Terrans had accepted as purest fantasy for centuries came into his mind. Could it be that his own world had its Foanna?

Ross scowled. You couldn't refute their "magic," call it by what scientific name you wished—hypnotism . . . teleporting. They got results, and the results were impressive. Now he remembered the warning the Foanna themselves had delivered hours earlier to the Rovers. There were limits to their abilities; because they were forced to draw on mental and physical energy, they could be exhausted. Thus, they had barriers, too.

Again Ross considered the subject of barriers. Karara had been able to meet the aliens, if not mind-to-mind, then in a closer way even than Ashe. The talent which tied her to the dolphins had in turn been a bond with the Foanna. Ashe and Karara could enter that circle, but not Ross Murdock. Along with his new separation from Ashe came that feeling of inferiority to bite on, and the taste was sour.

"This isn't going to be easy."

So Ashe was awake.

"What can they do?" Ross asked in return.

"I don't know. I don't believe that they can teleport an army into Baldy headquarters the way Torgul expects. And it wouldn't do such an army good to get there and then be outclassed by the weapons the Baldies might have," Ashe said.

Ross had a moment of warmth and comfort; he knew that tone of old. Ashe was studying the problem, willing to talk out difficulties as he always had before.

"No, outright assault isn't the answer. We'll have to know more about the enemy. One thing puzzles me: Why have the Baldies suddenly stepped up their timing?"

"What makes you think they have?"

"Well, according to the accounts I've heard, it's been about three or four planet years here since some off-world devices have been infiltrating the native civilization—"

"You mean such things as those attractors set up on the reef at Zahur's castle?" Ross remembered Loketh's story.

"Those, and other things. The refinements added to the engine power on these ships . . . Torgul said they spread from Rover fleet to fleet; no one's sure where they started. The Baldies began slowly, but they are speeding up now—those fairing attacks have all been recent. And this assault on the Foanna citadel blew up almost overnight on a flimsy excuse. Why the quick push after the slow beginning?"

"Maybe they decided the natives are easy pushovers and they no longer have to worry about any real opposition," Ross suggested.

"Could be. Self-confidence becoming arrogance when they didn't uncover any opponent strong enough to matter. Or else, they may be spurred by some need with a time limit. If we knew the reason for those pylons, we might guess their motives."

"Are you going to try to change the future?"

"That sounds arrogant, too. Can we if we wish to? We never dared to try it on Terra. And the risk may be worse than all our fears. Also, the choice is not ours."

"There's one thing I don't understand," Ross said. "Why did the Foanna walk out of the citadel and leave it undefended for their enemies? What about their guards? Did they just leave them too?" He was willing to make the most of any flaw in the aliens' character.

"Most of their people had already escaped through underground ways. The rest left when they knew the cutters had been sunk," Ashe returned. "As to why they deserted the citadel, I don't know. The decision was theirs."

There—up with the barrier between them again. But Ross refused to accept the cutoff this time, determined to pull Ashe back into the familiar world of the here and now.

"That keep could be a trap, about the best on this planet!" The idea was more than just a gambit to attract Ashe's attention, it was true! A perfect trap to catch Baldies.

"Don't you see?" Ross sat up, slapped his feet down on the deck as he leaned forward eagerly. "Don't you see . . . if the Baldies know anything at all about the Foanna, and I'm betting they do and want to learn all they can, they'll visit the citadel. They won't want to depend on second- and third-hand reports of the place, especially ones delivered by primitives such as the Wreckers. They had a sub there. I'll bet the crew are in picking over the loot right now!"

"If that's what they're hunting"—there was amusement in Ashe's tone—"they won't find much. The Foanna have better locks than their enemies have keys. You heard Ynlan before we left—any secrets left will remain secrets."

"But there's bait—bait for a trap!" argued Ross.

"You're right!" To the younger man's joy Ashe's enthusiasm was plain. "And if the Baldies could be led to believe that what they wanted was obtainable with just a little more effort, or the right tools—"

"The trap could net bigger catch than just underlings!" Ross's thought matched Ashe's. "Why, it might even pull in the VIP directing the whole operation! How can we set it up, and do we have time?"

"The trap would have to be of Foanna setting; our part would come after it was sprung." Ashe was thoughtful again. "But it is the only move which we can make at present with any hope of success. And it will only work if the Foanna are willing."

"Have to be done quickly," Ross pointed out.

"Yes, I'll see." Ashe was a dark figure against the thin light of the companionway as he slid back the cabin door. "If Ynvalda agrees . . ." As he went out Ross was right behind him.

The Foanna had been given, by their own choice, quarters on the bow deck of the cruiser where sailcloth had been used to form a tent. Not that any of the awe-stricken Rovers would venture too near them. Ashe reached for the flap of the fabric and a lilting voice called:

"You seek us, Gordoon?"

"This is important."

"Yes, it is important, for the thought which brings you both has merit. Enter then, brothers!"

The flap was looped aside and before them was a swirling of mist? . . . light? . . . sheets of pale color? Ross could not have described what he saw—save if the Foanna were there, he could not distinguish them from the rippling of their hair, the melting film of their robes.

"So, younger brother, you think that which was our

home and our treasure box has now become a trap for the confounding of those who believe we are a threat to them?"

Somehow Ross was not surprised that they knew about his idea before he had said a word, before Ashe had given any explanations. Their omniscience was only a small portion of their other talents.

"Yes."

"And why do you believe so? We swear to you that the coast folk can not be driven into those parts of the castle which mean the most, any more than our sea gate can be breached unless we will it so."

"Yet I swam through the sea gate, and the sub was there also." Ross knew again a flash of—was it pleasure? —at being able to state this fact. There *were* chinks in the Foanna defenses.

"Again the truth. You have that within you, young brother, which is both a lack and a shield. True also that this underseas ship entered after you. Perhaps it has a shield as part of it; perhaps those from the stars have their own protection. But they can not reach the heart of what they wish, not unless we open the doors for them. It is your belief, younger brother, that they will strive to force such doors?"

"Yes. Knowing there is something to be learned, they will try for it. They will not dare not to." Ross was very certain on that point. His encounters with the Baldies had not led to any real understanding. But the way they had wiped out the line of Russian time stations made him sure that they dealt thoroughly with any situation they considered a threat.

From the prisoners taken at Kyn Add they had learned the invaders believed the Foanna their enemies here, even though the Old Ones had not repulsed them or their activities. Therefore, it followed that, having taken the stronghold, the Baldies would endeavor to rip open every one of its secrets.

"A trap with good bait—"

Ross wondered which one of the Foanna said that. To see nothing but the swirls of mist-color, listen to disembodied voices from it, was disconcerting. Part of the stage dressing, he decided, for building their prestige with the other races with whom they dealt. Three women alone would have to buttress their authority with such trappings.

"Ah, younger brother, indeed you are beginning to understand us!" Laughter, soft, but unmistakable.

Ross frowned. He did not feel the touch-go-touch of mental communication which the dolphins used. But he did not doubt that the Foanna read his thoughts, or at least a few of them.

"Some of them," echoed from the mist. "Not all—not as your older brother's or the maiden whose mind meets with ours. With you, younger brother, it is a thought here, a thought there, and only our intuition to connect them into a pattern. But now, there is serious planning to be done. And, knowing this enemy, you believe they will come to search for what they can not find. So you would set a trap. But they have weapons beyond your weapons, have they not, younger brother? Brave as are these Rover kind, they can not use swords against flame, their hands against a killer who may stand apart and slay. What remains, Gordoon? What remains in our favor?"

"You have your weapons, too," Ashe answered.

"Yes, we have our weapons, but long have they been used only in one pattern, and they are attuned to another race. Did our defenses hold against you, Gordoon, when you strove to prove that you were as you claimed to be? And did another repulse younger brother when he dared the sea gate? So can we trust them in turn against these other strangers with different brains? Only at the testing shall we know, and in such learning perhaps we shall also be forced to eat the sourness of defeat. To risk all may be to lose all."

"That may be true," Ashe assented.

"You mean the sight you have had into our future says that this happens? Yes, to stake all and to lose—not only for ourselves, but for all others here—that is a weighty decision to make, Gordoon. But the trap promises. Let us think on it for a space. Do you also consult with the Rovers if they wish to take part in what may be desperate folly."

Torgul paced the afterdeck, well away from the tent which sheltered the Foanna, but with his eyes turning to it as Ross explained what might be a good attack.

"Those women-killers would have no fear of Foanna magic, rather would they come to seek it out? It would be a chance to catch leaders in a trap?"

"You have heard what the prisoners said or thought. Yes, they would seek out such knowledge and we would have this chance to capture them—"

"With what?" Torgul demanded. "I am not Ongal to argue that it is better to die in pursuit of blood payment than to take an enemy or enemies with me! What chance have we against their powers?"

"Ask that of them!" Ross nodded toward the still silent tent.

Even as he spoke the three cloaked Foanna emerged, pacing down to mid-ship where Torgul and his lieutenants, Ross and Ashe came to meet them.

"We have thought on this." The lilting half chant which the Foanna used for ordinary communication was a song in the dawn wind. "It was in our minds to retreat, to wait out this troubling of the land, since we are few and that which we hold within us is worth the guarding. But now, what profit such guardianship when there may be no one to whom we may pass it after us? And if you have seen the truth, elder brother"—the cowled heads swung to Ashe—"then there may be no future for any of us. But still there are our limitations. Rover," now they spoke directly to Torgul, "we can not put your men within the citadel by desiring—not without certain aids which lie sealed there now. No, we, ourselves, must win inside bodily and then . . . then, perhaps, we can pull tight the lines of our net!"

"To run a cruiser through the gate—" Torgul began.

"No, not a ship, Captain. A handful of warriors in the water can risk the gate, but not a ship."

Ashe broke in, "How many gill-packs do we have?"

Ross counted hurriedly. "I left one cached ashore. But there's mine and Karara's and Loketh's—also two more—"

"To pass the gates," that was the Foanna, "we ourselves shall not need your underwater aids."

"You," Ross said to Ashe, "and I with Karara's pack—"

"For Karara!"

Both the Terrans looked around. The Polynesian girl stood close to the Foanna, smiling faintly.

"This venture is mine also," she spoke with conviction. "As it is Tino-rau's and Taua's. Is that not so, Daughters of the Alii of this world?"

"Yes, Sea Maid. There are weapons of many sorts, and not all of them fit into a warrior's hand or can be swung with the force of a man's arm and shoulder. Yes, this venture is yours, also, sister."

Ross's protests bubbled unspoken; he had to accept the finality of the Foanna decree. It seemed now that the makeup of their task force depended upon the whims of the three rather than the experience of those trained to such risks. And Ashe was apparently willing to accept their leadership.

So it was an odd company that took to the water just as dawn colored the sky. Loketh had clung fiercely to his pack, insisted that he be one of the swimmers, and the Foanna accepted him as well. Ross and Ashe, Loketh, and Baleku, a young under officer of Ongal's, accorded the best swimmer of the fleet, Karara and the dolphins. And with them those three others, shapes sliding smoothly through the water, as difficult to define in this new element as they had been in their tent. Before them frisked the dolphins. Tino-rau and Taua played about the Foanna in an ecstatic joy and when all were in the sea they shot off shoreward.

That sub within the sea gate, had it unleashed the same lethal broadcast as the one at Kyn Add? But the dolphins could give warning if that were so.

Ross swam easily, Ashe next, Loketh on his left, Baleku a little behind and Karara to the fore as if in vain pursuit of the dolphins—the Foanna well to the left. A queer invasion party, even queerer when one totaled up the odds which might lie ahead.

There was no mist or storm this morning to hide the headlands where the Foanna citadel stood. And the promontories of the sea gate were starkly clear in the growing light. The same drive which always was a part of Ross when he was committed to action sustained him now, though he was visited by a small prick of doubt when he thought that the leadership did not lie with Ashe but with the Foanna.

No warning of any trouble ahead as they passed between the mighty, sea-sunk bases of the gate pillars. Ross depended upon his sonic, but there was no adverse report from the sensitive recorder. The terrible chill of the water during the night attack had been dissipated, but here and there dead sea things floated, being torn and devoured by hunters of the waves.

They were well past the pillars when Ross was aware that Loketh had changed place in the line, spurting ahead. After him went Baleku. They caught up with Karara, flashed past her.

Ross looked to Ashe, on to the Foanna, but saw nothing to explain the action of the two Hawaikans. Then his sonic beat out a signal from Ashe.

"Danger . . . follow the Foanna . . . left."

Karara had already changed her course to head in that direction. Ahead of her he could see Loketh and Baleku both still bound for the mid-point of the shore where the jetty and the sunken cutters were. Ashe passed before him, and Ross reluctantly followed orders.

A shelf rock reached out from the cliff wall, under it a dark opening. The Foanna sought this without hesitation, Ashe, Karara, and Ross following. Moments later they were out of the water where footing sloped back and up. Below them Tino-rau and Taua nosed the rise, their heads lifting out of the water as they "spoke." And Karara hastened to reply.

"Loketh . . . Baleku . . ." Ross began when he caught a mental stroke of anger so deadly that it was a chill lance into his brain. He faced the Foanna, startled and a little frightened.

"They will not come—now." A knob-crowned wand stretched out in the air, pointing to the upper reaches of the slope. "Nor can any of their blood—unless we win."

"What is wrong?" Ashe asked.

"You were right, very right, men out of time! These invaders are not to be lightly dismissed. They have turned one of our own defenses against us. Loketh, Baleku, all of their kind, can be made into tools for a master. They belong to the enemy now."

"And we have failed so early?" Karara wanted to know.

Again that piercing thrust of anger so vivid that it was no mere emotion but seemed a tangible force.

"Failed? No, not yet have we even begun to fight! You were very right; this is such an evil as must be faced and fought, even if we lose all in battle! Now we must do that which none of our own race has done for generations—we must open three locks, throw wide the Great Door, and seek out the Keeper of the Closed Knowledge!"

Light, a sharp ray sighting from the tip of the wand. And the Foanna following that beam, the three Terrans coming after . . . into the unknown.

## XVI

## THE OPENING OF THE GREAT DOOR

IT WAS NOT the general airlessness of the long-closed passage which wore on Ross's nerves, made Karara suddenly reach out and clasp fingers about the wrists of the two men she walked between; it was a crushing sensation of age, of a toll of years so long, so heavy, as to make time itself into a turgid flood which tugged at their bodies, mired their feet as they trudged after the Foanna. This sense of age, of a dead and heavy past, was so stifling that all three Terrans breathed in gasps.

Karara's breaths became sobs. Yet she matched her pace to Ashe and Ross, kept going. Ross himself had little idea of their surroundings, but one small portion of his brain asked answerless questions. The foremost being: Why did the past crush in on him here? He had traveled time, but never before had he been beaten with the feel of countless dead and dying years.

"Going back—" That hoarse whisper came from Ashe, and Ross thought he understood.

"A time gate!" He was eager to accept such an explanation. Time gates he could understand, but that the Foanna used one . . .

"Not our kind," Ashe replied.

But his words had pulled Ross out of a spell which had been as quicksand about him. And he began to fight back with a determination not to be sucked into what filled this place. In spite of Ross's efforts, his eyes could supply him with no definite impression of where they were. The ramp had led them out of the sea, but where they walked now, linked hand to hand, Ross could not say. He could see the glimmer of the Foanna; turning his head he could see his companions as shadows, but all beyond that was utter dark.

"Ahhhh—" Karara's sobs gave way to a whisper which was half moan. "This is a way of gods, old gods, gods who never dealt with men! It is not well to walk the road of the gods!"

Her fear lapped to Ross. He faced that emotion as he had faced so many different kinds of fear all his life. Sure, he felt that pressure on him, not the pressure of past centuries now—but a power beyond his ability to describe.

"Not our gods!" Ross put his stubborn defiance into words, more as a shield against his own wavering. "No power where there is no belief!" From what half-forgotten bit of reading had he dredged that knowledge? "No being without belief!" he repeated.

To his vast amazement he heard Ashe laugh, though the sound bordered on hysteria.

"No belief, no power," the older man replied. "You've speared the right fish, Ross! No gods of ours dwell here, Karara, and whatever god does has no rights over us. Hold to that, girl, hold tight!"

"Ye gods of sea, of sky, of woods,
Of mountains, of valleys,
Ye assemblies of gods,
Ye elder brothers of the gods that are,
Ye gods that once were,
Ye that whisper. Ye that watch by night,
Ye that show your gleaming eyes,
Come down, awake, stir,
Walk this road, walk this road!"

She was singing, first softly and then more strongly, the liquid words of her own tongue repeated in English as if what she strove to call she would share with her companions. Now there was triumph in her singing and

Ross found himself echoing her, "Walk this road!" as a demand.

It was still there, all of it, the crushing weight of the past, and that which brooded within that past, which had reached out for them, to possess or to alter. Only they were free of that reaching now. And they could see too! The fuzzy darkness was lighter and there were normal walls about them. Ross put out his free hand and rubbed fingertips along rough stone.

Once more their senses were assaulted by a stealthy attack from beyond the bounds of space and time as the walls fell away and they came out into a wide space whose boundaries they could not see. Here that which brooded was strong, a mighty weight poised aloft to strike them down.

"Come down, awake, stir . . ." Karara's pleading sank again to a whisper, her voice sounded hoarse as if her mouth were dry, her words formed by a shrunken tongue, issued from a parched throat.

Light spreading in channels along the floor, making a fiery pattern—patterns within patterns, intricate designs within designs. Ross jerked his eyes away from those patterns. To study them was danger, he knew without being warned. Karara's nails bit into his flesh and he welcomed that pain; it kept him alert, conscious of what was Ross Murdock, holding him safely apart from something greater than he, but entirely alien.

The designs and patterns were lines on a pavement. And now the three Foanna, swaying as if yielding to unseen winds, began to follow those patterns with small dancing steps. But the Terrans remained where they were, holding to one another for the sustaining strength their contact offered.

Back, forth, the Foanna danced—and once more their cloaks vanished or were discarded, so their silver-bright figures advanced, retreated, weaving a way from one arabesque to another. First about the outer rim and then in, by spirals and circles. No light except the crimson glowing rivulets on the floor, the silver bodies of the Foanna moving back and forth, in and out.

Then, suddenly, the three dancers halted, huddled together in an open space between the designs. And Ross was startled by the impression of confusion, doubt, almost despair wafted from them to the Terrans. Back across the patterned floor they came, their hands clasped even as the Terrans stood together, and now they fronted the three out of time.

"Too few . . . we are too few . . ." she who was the mid one of the trio said. "We can not open the Great Door."

"How many do you need?" Karara's voice was no longer parched, frightened. She might have traveled through fear to a new serenity.

Why did he think that, Ross wondered fleetingly. Was it because he, too, had had the same release?

The Polynesian girl loosed her grip on her companions' hands, taking a step closer to the Foanna.

"Three can be four—"

"Or five." Ashe moved up beside her. "If we suit your purpose."

Was Gordon Ashe crazy? Or had he fallen victim to whatever filled this place? Yet it was Ashe's voice, sane, serene, as Ross had always heard it. The younger Agent wet his lips; it was his turn to have a dry mouth. This was not his game; it could not be. Yet he summoned voice enough to add in turn:

"Six—"

When it came the Foanna answer was a warning.

"To aid us you must cast aside your shields, allow your identities to become one with our forces. Having done so, it may be that you shall never be as you are now but changed."

"Changed . . ."

The word echoed, perhaps not in the place where they stood, but in Ross's head. This was a risk such as he had never taken before. His chances in the past had been matters of action where his own strength and wits were matched against the problem. Here, he would open a door to forces he and his kind should not meet—expose himself to danger such as did not exist on the plane where weapons and strength of arm could decide victory or defeat.

And this was not really his fight at all. What did it matter to Terrans ten thousand years or so in the future what happened to Hawaikans in this past? He was a fool; they were all fools to become embroiled in this. The Baldies and their stellar empire—if that ever had existed as the Terrans surmised—were long gone before his breed entered space.

"If you accomplish that with our aid," said Ashe, "will you be able to defeat the invaders?"

Again a lengthening moment of silence before the Foanna replied.

"We can not tell. We only know that there is a force laid up here, set behind certain gates in the far past, upon which we may call for some supreme effort. But this much we also know: The Evil of the Shadow reaches out from here now, and where that darkness falls men will no longer be men but things in the guise of men who obey and follow as mindless creatures. As yet this shadow of the Shadow is a small one. But it will spread, for that is the nature of those who have spawned it. They have chanced upon and corrupted a thing we know. Such power feeds upon the will to power. Having turned it to their bidding, they will not be able to resist using it, for it is so easy to do and the results exult the nature of those who employ it.

"You have said that you and those like you who travel the time trails fear to change the past. Here the first steps have been taken to alter the future, but unless we complete the defense it will be ill for all of us."

"And this is your only weapon?" Ashe asked once more.

"The only one strong enough to stand against that which is now unleashed."

In the pavement the fiery lines were bright and glowing. Even when Ross shut his eyes, parts of those designs were still visible against his eyelids.

"We don't know how." He made a last feeble protest on the side of prudence. "We couldn't move as you did."

"Apart, no—together, yes."

The silvery figures were once more swaying, the mist which was their hair flowing about them. Karara's hands went out, and the slender fingers of one of the Foanna lifted, closed about firm, brown Terran flesh. Ashe was doing the same!

Ross thought he cried out, but he could not be sure, as he watched Karara's head begin to sway in concert with her Foanna partner, her black hair springing out from her shoulders to rival the rippling strands of the aliens'. Ashe was consciously matching steps with the companion who also drew him along a flowing line of fire.

In this last instant Ross realized the time for retreat was past—there was no place left to go. His hands went out, though he had to force that invitation because in him there was a shrinking horror of this surrender. But he could not let the others go without him.

The Foanna's touch was cool, and yet it seemed that flesh met his flesh, fingers as normal as his met fingers in that grasp. And when that hold was complete he gave a small gasp. For his horror was wiped away; he knew in its place a burst of energy which could be disciplined to use as a weapon or a tool in concentrated and complicated action. His feet so . . . and then so . . . Did those directions flow without words from the Foanna's fingers to his and then along his nerves to his brain? He only knew which was the proper next step, and the next, and the next, as they wove their way along the pattern lines, with their going adding a necessary thread to a design.

Forward four steps, backward one—in and out. Did Ross actually hear that sweet thrumming, akin to the lilting speech of the Foanna, or was it a throbbing in his blood? In and out . . . What had become of the others he did not know; he was aware only of his own path, of the hand in his, of the silvery shape at his side to whom he was now tied as if one of the Rover capture nets enclosed them both.

The fiery lines under his feet were smoking, tendrils rising and twisting as the hair of the Foanna rippled and twisted. And the smoke clung, wreathed his body. They moved in a cocoon of smoke, thicker and thicker, until Ross could not even see the Foanna who accompanied him, was only assured of her presence by the hand which grasped his.

And a small part of him clung desperately to the awareness of that clasp as an anchorage against what might come, a tie between the world of reality and the place into which he was passing.

How did one find words to describe this? Ross won dered with that part of him which remained stubbornly Ross Murdock, Terran Time Agent. He thought that he did not see with his eyes, hear with his ears but used other senses his own kind did not recognize or acknowledge.

Space . . . not a room . . . a cave—anything made by normal nature. Space which held something.

Pure energy? His Terran mind strove to give name to that which was nameless. Perhaps it was that spark of memory and consciousness which gave him that instant of "Seeing." Was it a throne? And on it a shimmering figure? He was regarded intently, measured, and —set aside.

There were questions or a question he could not hear, and perhaps an answer he would never be able to understand. Or had any of this happened at all?

Ross crouched on a cold floor, his head hanging, drained of energy, of all that feeling of power and well-being he had had when they had begun their dance across the symbols. About him those designs still glowed dully. When he looked at them too intently his head ached. He could almost understand, but the struggle was so exhausting he winced at the effort.

"Gordon—?"

There was no clasp on his hand; he was alone, alone between two glowing arabesques. That loneliness struck at him with the sharpness of a blow. His head came up; frantically he stared about him in search of his companions. "Gordon!" His plea and demand in one was answered:

"Ross?"

On his hands and knees, Ross used the rags of his strength to crawl in that direction, stopping now and then to shade his eyes with his hands, to peer through the cracks between his fingers for some sight of Ashe.

There he was, sitting quietly, his head up as if he were listening, or striving to listen. His cheeks were sunken; he had the drained, worn look of a man strained to the limit of physical energy. Yet there was a quiet peace in his face. Ross crawled on, put out a hand to Ashe's arm as if only by touching the other could he be sure he was not an illusion. And Ashe's fingers came up to cover the younger man's in a grasp as tight as the Foanna's hold had been.

"We did it; together we did it," Ashe said. "But where—why—?"

Those questions were not aimed at him, Ross knew. And at that moment the younger man did not care where they had been, what they had done. It was enough that his terrible loneliness was gone, that Ashe was here.

Still keeping his hold on Ross, Ashe turned his head and called into the wilderness of the symbol-glowing space about them, "Karara?"

She came to them, not crawling, not wrung almost dry of spirit and strength, but on her two feet. About her shoulders her dark hair waved and spun—or was it dark now? Along those strands there seemed to be threaded motes of light, giving a silvery sheen which was a faint echo of the Foanna's tresses. And was it only his bemused and bewildered sight, Ross mused, or was her skin fairer?

Karara smiled down at them and held out her hands, offering one to each. When they took them Ross knew again that surge of energy he had felt when he had followed the Foanna into the maze dance.

"Come! There is much to do."

He could not be mistaken; her voice held the singing lilt of the Foanna. Somehow she had crossed some barrier to become a paler, perhaps a lesser, but still a copy of the three aliens. Was this what they had meant when they warned of a change which might come to those who followed them into the ritual of this place?

Ross looked from the girl to Ashe with searching intensity. No, he could see no outward change in Gordon. And he felt none within himself.

"Come!" Some of Karara's old impetuousness returned as she tugged at them, urging them to their feet and drawing them with her. She appeared to know where they must go, and both men followed her guidance.

Once more they came out of the weird and alien into the normal, for here were the rock walls of a passage running up at an angle which became so steep they were forced to pull along by handholds hollowed in the walls.

"Where are we going?" She asked.

"To cleanse." Karara's answer was ambiguous, and she sped along hardly touching the handholds. "But hurry!"

They finished their climb and were in another corridor where patches of sunlight came through a pierced wall to dazzle their eyes. This was similar to the way which had run beside the courtyard in Zahur's castle.

Ross looked out of the first opening down into a courtyard. But where Zahur's had held the busy life of a castle, this was silent. Silent, but not deserted. There were men below, armed, helmed. He recognized the uniform of the Wrecker warriors, saw one or two who wore the gray of the Foanna servants. They stood in lines, unmoving, without speech among themselves, men who might have been frozen into immobility and arranged so for some game in which they were the voiceless, will-less pieces.

And their immobility was a thing to arouse fear. Were they dead and still standing?

"Come!" Karara's voice had sunk to a whisper and her hand pulled at the men.

"What–?" began Ross.

Ashe shook his head. Those rows below drawn up as if in order to march, unliving rows. They could not be alive as the Terrans knew life!

Ross left his vantage point, ready to follow Karara. But he could not blot from his mind the picture of those lines, nor forget the terrible blankness which made their faces more unhuman, more frighteningly alien than those of the Foanna.

## XVII

## SHADES AGAINST SHADOW

THE CORRIDOR ended in a narrow slit of room, and the wall before them was not the worked stone of the citadel but a single slab of what appeared to be glass curdled into creamy ridges and depressions.

Here were the Foanna, their robes once more cloaking them. Each held, point out, one of the rods. They moved slowly but with the precise gestures of those about a demanding and very important task as they traced each depression in the wall before them with the wand points. Down, up, around . . . as their feet had moved in the dance pattern, so now their wands moved to cover each line.

"Now!"

The wands dropped points to the floor. The Foanna moved equidistant from one another. Then, as one, the rods were lifted vertically, brought down together with a single loud tap.

On the wall the blue lines they had traced with such care darkened, melted. The glassy slab shivered, shattered, fell outward in a lace of fragments. So the narrow room became a balcony above a large chamber.

Below a platform ran the full length of that hall, and on it were mounted a line of oval disks. These had been turned to different angles and each reflected light, a ray beam directed at them from a machine whose metallic casing, projecting antennae, was oddly out of place here.

Once more the three staffs of the Foanna raised as one in the air. This time, from the knobs held out over the hall blazed, not the unusual whirl of small sparks, but strong beams of light—blue light darkening as it pierced downward until it became thrusting lines of almost tangible substance.

When those blue beams struck the nearest ovals they webbed with lines which cracked wide open. Shattered bits tinkled down to the platform. There was a stir at the end of the hall where the machine stood. Figures ran into plain sight. Baldies! Ross cried out a warning as he saw those star men raise weapon tubes aimed at the perch on which the Foanna stood.

Fire crackling with the speed and sound of lightning lashed up at the balcony. The lances of light met the spears of dark, and there was a flash which blinded Ross, a sound which split open the whole world.

The Terran's eyes opened, not upon darkness but on dazzling light, flashes of it which tore over him in great sweeping arcs. Dazed, sick, he tried to press his prone body into the unyielding surface on which he lay. But there was no way of burrowing out of this wild storm of light and clashing sound. Now under him the very fabric of the floor rocked and quivered as if it were being shaken apart into crumbling rubble.

All the will and ability to move was gone. Ross could only lie there and endure. What had happened, he did not know save that what raged about him now was a warring of inimical forces, perhaps both feeding on each other even as they strove for mastery.

The play of rays resembled sword blades crossing, fencing. Ross threw his arm over his eyes to shut out the intolerable brilliance of that thrust and counter. His body tingled and winced as the whirlwind of energy clashed and reclashed. He was beaten, stupid, as a man pinned down too long under a heavy shelling.

How did it end? In one terrific thunderclap of sound and blasting powder? And when did it end—hours . . . days later? Time was a thing set apart from this. Ross lay in the quiet which his body welcomed thirstily.

Then he was conscious of the touch of wind on his face, wind carrying the hint of sea salt.

He opened his eyes and saw above him a patch of clouded sky. Shakily he levered himself up on his elbows. There were no complete walls any more, just jagged points of masonry, broken teeth set in a skull's jawbone. Open sky, dark clouds, spattering rain.

"Gordon? Karara?" Ross's voice was a thin whisper. He licked his lips and tried again:

"Gordon!"

Had there been an answering whimper? Ross crawled into a hollow between two fallen blocks. A pool of water? No, it was the cloak of one of the Foanna spread out across the flooring in this fragment of room. Then Ross saw that Ashe was there, the cloaked figure braced against the Terran's shoulder as he half supported, half embraced the Foanna.

"Ynvalda!" Ashe called that with an urgency which was demanding. Now the Foanna moved, raising an arm in the cloak's flowing sleeve.

Ross sat back on his heels.

"Ross—Ashe?" He turned his head. Karara stood there, then came forward, planting her feet with care, her hands outstretched, her eyes wide and unseeing. Ross pulled himself up and went to her, finding that the once solid floor seemed to dip and sway under him, until he, too, must balance and creep. His hands closed on her shoulders and he pulled her to him in mutual support.

"Gordon?"

"Over there. You all right?"

"I think so." Her voice was weak. "The Foanna . . . Ynlan . . . Ynvalda—" Steadying herself against him, she tried to look around.

The place which had once been a narrow room, then a balcony, was now a perch above stomach-turning space. The hall of the oval mirrors was gone, having disappeared into a hollow the depths of which were veiled by a vapor which boiled and bubbled as if, far below, some huge caldron hung above a blazing fire.

Karara cried out and Ross drew her back from that drop. He was clearer-headed now and looked about for some way down from this doubtful perch. Of the other two Foanna there was no sign. Had they been sucked up and out in the inferno they had created with their unleashing of energy against the Baldies' installation?

"Ross—look!" Karara's cry, her upflung arm directed his attention aloft.

Under the sullen gathering of the storm a sphere arose as a bubble might seek the surface of a pool before breaking. A ship—a Baldy ship taking off from the ruined citadel! So some of the enemy had survived that trial of strength!

The globe was small, a scout used for within-atmosphere exploration, Ross judged. It arose first, and then moved inland, fleeing the gathering storm, to be out of sight in moments. Inland, where the mountain base of the invaders was reputed to be. Retreating? Or bound to gather reinforcements?

"Baldies?" Karara asked.

"Yes."

She wiped her hand across her face, smearing dust and grime on her cheeks. As raindrops pattered about them Ross drew the girl with him into the alcove where Ashe sheltered with the Foanna. The cowled alien was sitting up, her hand still gripping one of the wands, now a half-melted ruin.

Ashe glanced at them as if for the first time he remembered they might be there.

"Baldy ship just took off inland," Ross told him. "We didn't see either of the other Foanna."

"They have gone to do what is to be done," Ashe's companion replied. "So some of the enemy fled. Well, perhaps they have learned one lesson, not to meddle with others' devices. Ahh, so much gone which will never come again! Never again—"

She held up the half-melted wand, turning it back and forth before her, before she cast it away. It flew out, up, then dropped into the caldron of the hall which had been. A gust of rain, cold, chilling the lightly clad Terrans, swept across them.

The Foanna was helped to her feet by Ashe. For a moment she turned slowly, giving a lingering look to the ruins. Then she spoke: "Broken stone holds no value. Take hands, my brothers, my sister, it is time we go hence."

Karara's hand in Ross's right, Ashe's in his left, and both linked to Ynvalda in turn. Then—they were indeed elsewhere, in a courtyard where bodies lay flaccid under the drenching downpour of the rain. And moving among those bodies were the two other Foanna, bending to examine one man after another. Perhaps over one in three they so inspected they held consultation before a wand was used in tracing certain portions of the body between them. When they were finished, that man stirred, moaned, showed signs of life once more.

"Ross—!" From behind a tumbled wall crept a Hawaikan who did not wear the guard armor of the others. Gill-pack, flippers, diver's belt, had been stripped from him. There was a bleeding gash down the side of his face, and he held his left arm against his body, supported by his right hand.

"Baleku!"

The Rover pulled himself up to his feet and stood swaying. Ross reached him quickly to catch him as he slumped forward.

"Loketh?" the Terran asked.

"The women-killers took him." Somehow the Rover got that out as Ross half supported, half led him to where the Foanna were gathering those they had been able to revive. "They wanted to learn"—Baleku was obviously making a great effort to tell his story—"about . . . about where we came from . . . where we got the packs."

"So now they will know of us, or will if they get the story out of Loketh." Ashe worked with Ross to splint the Rover's broken arm. "How many of them were here, Baleku?"

The Rover's head moved slowly from side to side. "I do not know the truth. It is—was—like a dream. I was in the water swimming through the sea gate. Then suddenly I was in another place where those from the stars waited about me. They had our packs and belts and these they showed us, demanding to know whereof these were. Loketh was like one deep in sleep and they left him so when they questioned me. Then there came a great noise and the floor under us shook, lightning flashed through the air. Two of the women-killers ran from the room and all of them were greatly excited. They took up Loketh and carried him away, with him the packs and other things. And I was left alone, though I could not move—as if they had left me in a net I could not see.

"More and more were the flashes. Then one of those slayers of women stood in the doorway. He raised his hand, and my feet were free, but I could not move otherwise than to follow after him. We came along a hall and into this court where men stood unstirring, although stones fell from the walls upon some of them and the ground shook—"

Baleku's voice grew shriller, his words ran together. "The one who pulled me after him by his will—he cried out and put his hands to his head. Back and forth he ran, bumping into the standing men, and once running into a wall as if he were blinded. And then he was gone and I was alone. There was more falling stone and one struck my shoulder so I was thrown to the ground. There I lay until you came."

"So few—out of many so few—" One of the Foanna stood beside them, her cloak streaming with the falling rain. "And for these"—she faced the lines of those they had not revived—"there was no chance. They died as helplessly as if they went into a meeting of swords with their arms bound to their sides! Evil have we wrought here."

Ashe shook his head. "Evil has been wrought here, Ynlan, but not by your seeking. And those who died here helplessly may be only a small portion of those yet to be sacrificed. Have you forgotten the slaughter at Kyn Add and those other fairings where women and children were also struck down to serve some purpose we do not even yet know?"

"Lady, Great One—" Baleku struggled to sit up and Ross slipped an arm beside him in aid. "She for whom I made a bride-cup was meat for them at Kyn Add, along with many others. If these slayers are not put to the sword's edge, there will be other fairings so used. And these Shadow ones possess a magic to draw men to them helplessly to be killed. Great One, you have powers; all men know that wind and wave obey your call. Do you now use your magic! It is better to fall with a power we know, than answer such spells as those killers have netted about the men here!"

"This is one weapon which they shall not use again." Ynvalda rose from a stone block where she had been sitting. "And perhaps in its way it was one of the most dangerous. But in defeating it we have by so much weakened ourselves also. And the strong place of these star men lies not on the coast, but inland. They will be warned by those who fled this place. Wind and wave, yes, those have served our purpose in the past. But now perhaps we have found that which our power will not best! Only—for this"—her gesture was for the ruins of the citadel and the dead—"there shall be a payment exacted—to the height of our desire!"

Whether the Foanna did have any control over the storm winds or not, the present deluge appeared not to accommodate them. The dazed, injured survivors of the courtyard were brought to shelter in some of the underground passages.

There appeared to be no other reminders of the Wrecker force which had earlier besieged the keep than those survivors. But within hours some of those who had served the Foanna for generations returned. And the Foanna themselves opened the sea gates so that the Rover cruisers anchored in the small bay below their ruined walls.

A small force, and one ill-equipped to go up against the Baldies. Some five star men's bodies had been found in the citadel, but the ship had gone off to warn their base. To Ross's thinking the advantage still lay with the invaders.

But the Hawaikans refused to accept the idea that the odds were against them. As soon as the storm blew out its force Ongal's cruiser headed northward to other clan fairings where the Rovers could claim kinship. And Afrutka sailed on the same errand south. While some of the Wreckers were released to carry the warning to their lords. Just how great a force could be gathered through such means and how effective it would be, was a question to make the Terrans uneasy.

Karara disappeared with the Foanna into the surviving inner cliff-burrows below the citadel. But Ashe and Ross remained with Torgul and his officers, striving to bring organization out of the chaos about them.

"We must know just where their lair lies," Torgul stated the obvious. "The mountains you believe, and they can fly in sky ships to and from that point. Well"—he spread out a chart—"here are the mountains on this island, running so. An army marching hither could be sighted from sky ships. Also, there are many mountains. Which is the one or ones we must seek? It may take many tens of days to find that place, while they will always know where we are, watch us from above, prepare for our coming—"

Again Ross mentally paid tribute to the Captain's quick grasp of essentials.

"You have a solution, Captain?" Ashe asked.

"There is the river—here—" Torgul said reflectively. "Perhaps I think in terms of water because I am a sailor. But here it does run, and for this far along it our cruisers may ascend." He pointed with his fingertip. "This lies, however, in Glicmas's land, and he is now the mightiest of the Wrecker lords, his sword always drawn against us. I do not believe that we could talk him into—"

"Glicmas!" Ross interrupted. They both looked at him inquiringly, and he repeated Loketh's story of the Wrecker lord who had had dealings with a "voice from the mountain" and so gained the wrecking devices to make him the dominant lord of the district.

"So!" Torgul exclaimed. "That is the evil of this Shadow in the mountains! No, under those circumstances I do not think we shall talk Glicmas into furthering any raid against those who have made him great over his fellows. Rather will he turn against us in their cause."

"And if we do not use the cruisers up the river"—Ashe conned the map—"then perhaps a small party or parties working overland could strike the stream here, nearer to the uplands."

Torgul frowned at the map. "I do not think so. Even small parties moving in that direction would be sighted by Glicmas's people. The more so if they headed inland. He will not wish to share his secrets with others."

"But, say—a party of Foanna."

The Captain glanced up swiftly to favor Ashe with a keen regard. "Then he would not dare. No, I am sure he would not dare to interfere. Not yet has he risen high enough to turn the hook of his sword against them. But would the Foanna do so?"

"If not the Foanna, the others wearing like robes," Ashe said slowly.

"Others wearing like robes?" repeated Torgul. Now his frown was heavy. "No man would take on the guise of the Foanna; he would be blasted by their power for so doing. If the Foanna will lead us in their persons, then we shall follow gladly, knowing that their magic will be with us."

"There is also this," Ross broke in. "The Baldies have the gill-packs they took from Baleku and Loketh, and they have Loketh. They will want to learn more about us. We hoped that the citadel would provide bait to draw them and it did. That our plan for a trap there was spoiled was ill fortune. But I am sure that if the Baldies believe we are coming to them, they will hold off an all-out attack against our march, hoping to gather us in intact. They'd risk that."

Ashe nodded. "I agree. We are the unknown they must solve now. And this much I am sure of—the future of this world and her people balances on a very narrow line of choice. It is my hope that such a choice is still to be made."

Torgul smiled thinly. "We live in perilous times when the Shades require our swords to go up against the Shadow!"

## XVIII

## WORLD IN DOUBT?

THE DAY WAS dully overcast as all days had been since they had begun this sulk-and-march penetration into the mountain territory. Ross could not accept the idea that the Foanna might actually command wind and wave, storm and sun, as the Hawaikans firmly believed, but the gloomy weather *had* favored them so far. And now they had reached the last breathing point before they took the plunge into the heart of the enemy country. About the way in which they were to make that plunge, Ross had his own plan. One he did not intend to share with either Ashe or Karara. Though he had had to outline it to the one now waiting here with him.

"This is still your mind, younger brother?"

He did not turn his head to look at the cloaked figure. "It is still my mind!" Ross could be firm on that point.

The Terran backed out of the vantage place from which he had been studying the canyonlike valley cupping the Baldy spaceship. Now he got to his feet and faced Ynlan, his own gray cloak billowing out in the wind to reveal the Rover scale armor underneath.

"You can do it for me?" he asked in turn. During the past days the Foanna had admitted that the weird battle within the citadel had weakened and limited their "magic." Last night they had detected a force barrier ahead and to transport the whole party through that by teleporting was impossible.

"Yes, you alone. Then my wand would be drained for a space. But what can you do within their hold, save be meat for their taking?"

"There can not be too many of them left there. That's a small ship. They lost five at the citadel, and the Rovers have three prisoners. No sign of the scout ship we know they have—so more of them must be gone in it. I won't be facing an army. And what they have in the way of weapons may be powered by installations in the ship. A lot of damage done there. Or even if the ship lifted—" He was not sure of what he could do; this was a venture depending largely on improvisation at the last moment.

"You propose to send off the ship?"

"I don't know whether that is possible. No, perhaps I can only attract their attention, break through the force shield so the rest may attack."

Ross knew that he must attempt this independent action, that in order to remain the Ross Murdock he had always been, he must be an actor not a spectator.

The Foanna did not argue with him now. "Where—?" Her long sleeve rippled as she gestured to the canyon. Dull as the skies were overhead, there was light here—too much of it for his purpose as the ground about the ship was open. To appear there might be fatal.

Ross was grasped by another and much more promising idea. The Foanna had transported them all to the deck of Torgul's cruiser after asking him to picture it for her mentally. And to all outward appearances the Baldy ship before them now was twin to the one which had taken him once on a fantastic voyage across a long-vanished stellar empire. Such a ship he knew!

"Can you put me in the ship?"

"If you have a good memory of it, yes. But how know you these ships?"

"I was in one once for many days. If these are alike, then I know it well!"

"And if this is unlike, to try such may mean your death."

He had to accept her warning. Yet outwardly this ship was a duplicate. And before he had voyaged on the derelict he had also explored a Wrecker freighter on his own world thousands of years before his own race had evolved. There was one portion of both ships which had been identical—save for size—and that part was the best for his purpose.

"Send me—here!"

With closed eyes, Ross produced a mental picture of the control cabin. Those seats which were not really seats but webbing support swinging before banks of buttons and levers; all the other installations he had watched, studied, until they were as known to him as the plate bulkheads of the cabin below in which he had slept. Very vivid, that memory. He felt the touch of the Foanna's cool fingers on his forehead—then it was gone. He opened his eyes.

No more wind and gloom, he stood directly behind the pilot's web-sling, facing a vista-plate and rows of controls, just as he had stood so many times in the derelict. He had made it! This was the control cabin of the spacer. And it was alive—the faint thrumming in the air, the play of lights on the boards.

Ross pulled the cowl of his Foanna cloak up over his head. He had had days to accustom himself to the bulk of the robe, but still its swathings were sometimes a hindrance rather than a help. Slowly he turned. There were no Baldies here, but the well door to the lower levels was open, and from it came small sounds echoing up the communication ladder. The ship was occupied.

Not for the first time since he had started on this venture Ross wished for more complete information. Doubtless several of those buttons or levers before him controlled devices which could be the greatest aid to him now. But which and how he did not know. Once in just such a cabin he had meddled and, in activating a long silent installation, had called the attention of the Baldies to their wrecked ship, to the Terrans looting it. Only by the merest chance had the vengeance of the stellar spacemen fallen then on the Russian investigators and not on his own people.

He knew better than to touch anything before the pilot's station, but the banks of controls to one side were concerned with the inner well-being of the ship—and they tempted him. To go it blind was, however, more of a risk than he dared to take. There was one future precaution for him.

From a very familiar case beside the pilot's seat Ross gathered up a collection of disks, sorted through them hastily for one which bore a certain symbol on its covering. There was only one of those. Slapping the rest back into their container, Ross pressed a button on the control board.

Again his guess paid off! Another disk was exposed as a small panel slid back. Ross clawed that out of the holder, put in its place the one he had found. Now, if his choice had been correct, the crew who took off in this ship, unless they checked their route tape first, would find themselves heading to another primitive planet and not returning to base. Perhaps exhaustion of fuel might ground them past hope of ever regaining their home port again. Next to damaging the ship, which he could not do, this was the best thing to assure that any enemy leaving Hawaika would not speedily return with a second expeditionary force.

Ross dropped the route disk he had taken out into a pocket on his belt, to be destroyed when he had the chance. Now he catfooted across the deck to look into the well and listen.

The walls glowed with a diffused light. From here the Terran could count at least four levels under him, with perhaps another. The bottom two ought to be supplies and general storage. Then the engine room, tech labs above, and next to the control cabin the living quarters.

Through the fabric of the ship, shivering up his body from the soles of his feet, he could feel the vibration of engines at work. One such must control the force field which ringed this canyon, perhaps even powered the weapons the invaders could turn against any assault.

Ross whirled about, his Foanna cloak in a wide swing. There was one control which he knew. Yes, again the board was the same as the one he was familar with. His hand plunged out and down, raking the lever from one measure point to the very end of the slit in which it moved. Then he planted himself with his back to the wall. Whoever came up the well hunting the cause for the failure would be facing the other way. Ross crouched a little, pushing the cape well back on his shoulders to free his arms. There was a feline suppleness in his stance just as a jungle cat might wait coming of its prey.

What he heard was a shout below, the click of footgear on the rungs of the level ladder. Ross's lips drew back in a snarl which was also feline. He thought that would do it! Spacemen were ultra-sensitive to any failure in air flow.

White head, bare of any hair, thin shoulders a little hunched under the blue-green-lavender stuff of the Baldies' uniforms . . . Head turning now so that the eyes could see the necessary switch. An exclamation from the alien and—

But the Baldy never had a chance to complete that turn, look behind him. Ross sprang and struck with the side of his hand. The hairless head snapped forward. His hands already hooked in the other's armpits, the Terran heaved the alien up and over onto the deck of the control cabin. It was only when he was about to bind his captive that Ross discovered the Baldy was dead. A blow calculated to stun the alien had been too severe. Breathing a little faster, the Terran rolled the body back and hoisted it into the navigator's swing-seat, fastening it with the takeoff belts. One down—how many left?

He had little time to wonder, for before he could

reach the well once again there was a call from below—sharp and demanding. The Terran searched his victim, but the Baldy was unarmed.

Again a shout. The silence—too complete a silence. How could they have guessed trouble so quickly? Unless, unless the Baldies' mental communication had been at work . . . they might even now know their fellow was dead.

But not how he died. Ross was prepared to grant the Baldies super-Terran abilities, but he did not see how they could know what had happened here. They could only suspect danger, not know the form it had taken. And sooner or later one of them must come to adjust the switch. This could be a duel of patience.

Ross squatted at the edge of the well, trying to make his ears supply him with hints of what might be happening below. Had there been an alteration in the volume of vibration? He set his palm flat to the deck, tried to deduce the truth. But he could not be sure. That there had been some slight change he was certain.

They could not wait much longer without making an attempt to reopen the air-supply regulator, or could they? Again Ross was hampered by lack of information. Perhaps the Baldies did not need the same amount of oxygen his own kind depended upon. And if that were true, Ross could be the first to suffer in playing a waiting game. Well, air was not the only thing he could cut off from here, though it had been the first and most important to his mind. Ross hesitated. Two-edged weapons cut in both directions. But he had to force a countermove from them. He pulled another switch. The control cabin, the whole of the ship, was plunged into darkness.

No sound from below this time. Ross pictured the interior layout of the ships he had known. Two levels down to reach the engine room. Could he descend undetected? There was only one way to test that—try it.

He pulled the Foanna cloak about him, was several rungs down the ladder when the glow in the walls came on. An emergency switch? With a forward scramble, Ross swung into one of the radiating side corridors. The sliding-door panels along it were all closed; he could detect no sounds behind them. But the vibration in the ship's wall had returned to its steady beat.

Now the Terran realized the folly of his move. He was more securely trapped here than he had been in the control cabin. There was only one way out, up or down the ladder, and the enemy could have that under observation from below. All they would need to do was to use a flamer or a paralyzing ray such as the one he had turned over to Ashe several days ago.

Ross inched along to the stairwell. A faint pad of movement, a shadow of sound from the ladder. Someone on the way up. Could they mentally detect him, know him for an alien intruder by the broadcast of his thoughts? The Baldies had a certain respect for the Foanna and might desire to take one alive. He drew the robe about him, used it to muffle his figure completely as the true wearers did.

But the figure pulling painfully up from rung to rung was no Baldy. The lean Hawaikan arms, the thin Hawaikan face, drawn of feature, painfully blank of expression—Loketh—under the same dread spell as had held the warriors in the citadel courtyard. Could the aliens be using the Hawaikan captive as a defense shield, moving up behind him?

Loketh's head turned, those blank eyes regarded Ross. And their depths were troubled, recognition of a sort returning. The Hawaikan threw up one hand in a beseeching gesture and then went to his knees in the corridor.

"Great One! Great One!" The words came from his lips in a breathy hiss as he groveled. Then his body went flaccid, and he sprawled face down, his twisted leg drawn up as if he would run but could not.

"Foanna!" The one word came out of the walls themselves, or so it seemed.

"Foanna—the wise learn what lies before them when they walk alone in the dark." The Hawaikan speech was stilted, accented, but understandable.

Ross stood motionless. Had they somehow seen him through Loketh's eyes? Or had they been alerted merely by the Hawaikan's call? They believed he was one of the Foanna. Well, he would play that role.

"Foanna!" Sharper this time, demanding. "You lie in our hand. Let us clasp the fingers tightly and you shall be naught."

Out of somewhere the words Karara had chanted in the Foanna temple came to Ross—not in her Polynesian tongue but in the English she had repeated. And softening his voice to his best approximation of the Foanna singsong Ross sang:

> "Ye forty thousand gods,
> Ye gods of sea, of sky—of stars," he improvised.
> "Ye elders of the gods that are,
> Ye gods that once were,
> Ye that whisper, yet that watch by night,
> Ye that show your gleaming eyes."

"Foanna!" The summons was on the ragged edge of patience. "Your tricks will not move our mountains!"

"Ye gods of mountains," Ross returned, "of valleys, of Shades and not the Shadow," he wove in the beliefs of this world, too. "Walk now this world, between the stars!" His confidence was growing. And there was no use in remaining pent in this corridor. He would have to chance that they were not prepared to kill summarily one of the Foanna.

Ross went to the well, went down the ladder slowly, keeping his robe about him. Here at the next level there was a wider space about the opening, and three door panels. Behind one must be those he sought. He was buoyed up by a curious belief in himself, almost as if wearing this robe did give him in part the power attributed to the Foanna.

He laid his hand on the door to his right and sent it snapping back into its frame, stepped inside as if he entered here by right.

There were three Baldies. To his Terran eyes they were all superficially alike, but the one seated on a control stool had a cold arrogance in his expression, a pitiless half smile which made Ross face him squarely. The Terran longed for one of the Foanna staffs and the ability to use it. To spray that energy about this cabin might reduce the Baldy defenses to nothing. But now two of the paralyzing tubes were trained on him.

"You have come to us, Foanna, what have you to offer?" demanded the commander, if that was his rank.

"Offer?" For the first time Ross spoke. "There is no reason for the Foanna to make any offer, slayer of women and children. You have come from the stars to take, but that does not mean we choose to give."

He felt it now, that inner pulling, twisting in his mind, the willing which was their more subtle weapon. Once they had almost bent him with that willing because then he had worn their livery, a spacesuit taken from the wrecked freighter. Now he did not have that chink in his defense. And all that stubborn independence and determination to be himself alone resisted the influence with a fierce inner fire.

"We offer life to you, Foanna, freedom of the stars. These other dirt creepers are nothing to you, why take you weapons in their cause? You are not of the same race."

"Nor are you!" Ross's hands moved under the envelope of the robe, unloosing the two hidden clasps which held it. That bank of controls before which the commander sat—to silence that would cause trouble. And he depended upon Ynlan. The Rovers should now be massed at either end of the canyon waiting for the force field to fail and let them in.

Ross steadied himself, poised for action. "We have something for you, star men—" he tried to hold their attention with words, "have you not heard of the power of the Foanna—that they can command wind and wave? That they can be where they were not in a single movement of the eyelid? And this is so—behold!"

It was the oldest trick in the world, perhaps on any planet. But because it was so old maybe it had been forgotten by the aliens. For, as Ross pointed, those heads did turn for an instant.

He was in the air, the robe gathered in his arms wide spread as bat wings. And then they crashed in a tangle which bore them all back against the controls. Ross strove to enmesh them in the robe, using the pressure of his body to slam them all on the buttons and levers of the board. Whether that battering would accomplish his purpose, he could not tell. But that he had only these few seconds torn out of time to try, he knew, and determined to use them as best he could.

One of the Baldies had slithered down to the floor and another was aiming strangely ineffectual blows at him. But the third had wriggled free to bring up a paralyzer. Ross slewed around, dragging the alien he held across his body just as the other fired. But though the fighter went limp and heavy in Ross's hold, the Terran's own right arm fell to his side, his upper chest was numb, and his head felt as if one of the Rover's boarding axes had clipped it. Ross reeled back and fell, his left hand raking down the controls as he went. Then he lay on the cabin floor and saw the convulsed face of the commander above him, a paralyzer aiming at his middle.

To breathe was an effort Ross found torture to endure. The red haze in his head filled all the world. Pain —he strove to flee the pain but was held captive in it. And always the pressure on him kept that agony steady.

"Let . . . be . . ." He wanted to scream that. Perhaps he had, but the pressure continued. Then he forced his eyes open. Ashe—Ashe and one of the Foanna bending over him, Ashe's hands on his chest, pressing, relaxing, pressing again.

"It is good—" He knew Ynvalda's voice. Her hand rested lightly on his forehead and from that touch Ross drew again the quickening of body and spirit he had felt on the dancing floor.

"How—?" He began and then changed to—"Where—?" For this was not the engine room of the spacer. He lay in the open, with sweet, rain-wet wind filling his starved lungs now without Ashe's force aid.

"It is over," Ashe told him, "all over—for now."

But not until the sun reached the canyon hours later and they sat in council, did Ross learn all the tale. Just as he had made his own plan for reaching the spacer, so had Ashe, Karara, and the dolphins worked on a similar attempt. The river running deep in those mountain gorges had provided a road for the dolphins and they found beneath its surface an entrance past the force barrier.

"The Baldies were so sure of their superiority on this primitive world they set no guards save that field," Ashe explained. "We slipped through five swimmers to reach the ship. And then the field went down, thanks to you."

"So I did help—that much." Ross grinned wryly. What had he proven by his sortie? Nothing much. But he was not sorry he had made it. For the very fact he had done it on his own had eased in part that small ache which was in him now when he looked at Ashe and remembered how it had once been. Ashe might be—always would be—his friend, but the old tight-locking comradeship of the Project was behind them, vanished like the time gate.

"And what will you do with them?" Ross nodded toward the captives, the three from the ship, two more taken from the small scouting globe which had homed to find their enemies ready for them.

"We wait," Ynvalda said, "for those on the Rover ship

to be brought hither. By our laws they deserve death."

The Rovers at that council nodded vigorously, all save Torgul and Jazia. The Rover woman spoke first.

"They bear the Curse of Phutka heavy on them. To live under such a curse is worse than a clean, quick dying. Listen, it has come upon me that better this curse not only eat them up but be carried by them to rot those who sent them—"

Together the Foanna nodded. "There has been enough of killing," said Ynlan. "No, warriors, we do not say this because we shrink from rightful deaths. But Jazia speaks the truth in this matter. Let these depart. Perhaps they will bear that with them which will convince their leaders that this is not a world they may squeeze in their hands as one crushes a ripe quaya to eat its seeds. You believe in your cursing, Rovers, then let the fruit of it be made plain beyond the stars!"

Was this the time to speak of the switched tapes, Ross wondered. No, he did not really believe that the Rover curse or their treatment of the captives would, either one, influence the star leaders. But, if the invaders did not return to their base, their vanishing might also work to keep another expedition from invading Hawaikan skies. Leave it to chance, a curse, and time . . .

So it was decided.

"Have we won?" Ross asked Ashe later.

"Do you mean, have we changed the future? Who can answer that? They may return in force, this may have been a step which was taken before. Those pylons may still stand in the future above a deserted sea and island. We shall probably never know."

That was also their own truth. For them also there had been a substitution of journey tapes by Fate, and this was now their Hawaika. Ross Murdock, Gordon Ashe, Karara Trehern, Tino-rau, Taua—five Terrans forever lost in time, in the past with a dubious future. Would this be the barren, lotus world, or another now? Yes, no—either. They had found their key to the mystery out of time, but they could not turn it, and there was no key to the gate which had ceased to exist. Grasp tight the present. Ross looked about him. Yes, the present, which might be very satisfying after all. . . .